THE SECRET

NEVER SHARED

A Novel

THE SECRET NEVER SHARED

by

James H. Dove

Published by JHZ Publishing

Copyright © 2011 by James H. Dove

Printed Version ISBN-13: 978-0615588162

ISBN-10: 0615588166

EPUB Edition ISBN: 978-1-4524-6748-1

Printed in the USA

Bluffton, SC 29909

Table of Contents

Author's Note

This book is a work of fiction. All characters, places, events and organizations described in this novel are either used fictitiously or a product of the author's imagination.

I am deeply thankful to Professor William Decker, a perceptive scholar of English Literature and Composition at Roberts Wesleyan College, Reverend Dr. Jerry Kramer, Honorably Retired Presbyterian USA Pastor, and Ms. Sherry McKnight, my dedicated editor, all of whom served in church administration, for their considerable help with this novel. Each of these individuals served over forty years in dedicated Christian service and guided me with the characters' development, story flow and theological issues.

Mr. Charles Martin, an established author, helpfully provided publishing ideas along with encouragement. Additionally, I want to give special thanks to Bonnie, my patient and dedicated wife of forty-six years. She edited, encouraged and critiqued this work from the beginning. Without their help, advice and support, *The Secret Never Shared* would not have been completed.

The cover and the epilogue designs were created by Ms. Katrina D. Joyner. The cover photo of Peyto Lake is used by permission of Dreamstime.com and copyrighted by Skylightpictures. All other photographs were taken by the author or Bonnie K. Dove.

This book is dedicated to my children, Jim and Jennifer, and to my fabulous granddaughters, Hannah Dove, an aspiring young author and Zaina Dove, a talented young artist. Children like Hannah and Zaina help make life enjoyable for their parents and grandparents. They are our future.

Chapter 1
Remembering Dovie

Penny Stevens was sitting in the chapel, the same beautiful Harbison Chapel where she was married forty-six years ago today. Just yesterday, she reviewed her ancient wedding pictures in the frayed album she hadn't seen for several years. As Penny turned the pages with the slightly faded images, it was apparent 1965 styles were significantly different and perhaps more elegant than today's formal attire. The photos were mostly black and white with a few color images of the wedding party only.

The chapel still retains the same arching hand crafted woodwork reaching for the heavens, along with the precision stained-glass windows the camera recorded so many years ago. The colorful jewel-like windows command the sun to make remarkably strange geometric patterns with stunning, refracted and reflected light as it dances on the dark oak pews, gray stone arches and pale white walls. The roof, supported by massive, stained, wooden beams, absorbed what little light was available from the stained-glass and chain hung cylindrical lights. The Teaching Window which honors the world's greatest teachers has Christ at its center, and when entering the chapel attracts the eye with vivid colors. The masterpiece includes Moses,

Socrates, Pasteur, and Galileo along with New Testament writers Matthew, Mark, Luke and John.

Orchestrated by professors and students alike, the old four manual Kimball organ gloriously still brings forth, creatively arranged canticles for God and human's ears alike, as a professor coaches a group of talented musicians. Today, a charming female trio, is rehearsing a classical aria with a four-piece string orchestra for a forthcoming concert. The melodies are familiar to Penny, but the voices are new, probably freshman music majors preparing for careers in teaching or perhaps the performing arts. They exude confidence as they harmoniously animate the joyous words flowing from the enchanting Italian aria.

Penny's Dovie had died, forever gone from her until they meet again, on that beautiful shore, when her sorrow ceases and joy will triumphantly replace her despair. Her broken heart mourns her Dovie, the only man she ever loved, the only man she ever kissed. Her spirited and compassionate husband, lover and best friend left this world only twenty-nine days ago, but it seems like an eternity, and her enjoyment of life gone without him, — yes, totally finished! She recalled how they hugged each other every morning, pledging their love until the end of time, and now each hour seems an eternity as Penny dreads her future of loneliness. Their time together was truly extraordinary, for they genuinely loved one another. They comforted friends and relatives when heartbreaks or losses occurred in their lives, and they honored and served their living God. Penny asks,"what now?" How can Penny endure her broken heart and emptiness, even for another hour?

Each morning when Penny first stirs, she reaches out to touch Dove's hand or place her head on his breast, until she suddenly remembers he passed away, and she is companionless. Then the loneliness sets in again to torment Penny's soul for another day of grief. Occasionally, she calls to him, expecting Dove is toiling in his library scratching out some beautiful passage for an upcoming novel, but her soft voice echoes in the large, empty house that was their home. Nights are unbearable when she tosses and turns, totally unable to remove him from her consciousness. Penny struggles to put another day behind her, but she longs for the gentle touch of his giant, warm hand encompassing her dainty fingers, and the caress of his tender kiss from his satisfying lips as they embrace.

Will these moments, hours and days of anguish continue forever? Will she never rest? As Penny sits alone in this exquisite Grove City College chapel remembering the proud, generous and handsome man who uplifted and encouraged her for all those years, she now recalls the ancient gravestone she and Dove visited in Ireland. Penny recalls that weather-worn tomb that read, "Death leaves a heartache no one can heal, love leaves a memory no one can steal." More than any others, these words revealed Penny's pain and love, all at the same time.

Silently, as Penny sits on the darkly stained oak pew and reflects on their lengthy and blessed life together, she prays for reinvigorated strength to march forward and for added courage to continue the work Dove and she started so many years ago. First, however, Penny must remember and rejoice celebrating the memories of the ample marvelous experiences, the abundance of proud moments and the unimaginable joy she and Dovie shared together for those forty-six incredible years. How can Penny endure a life without his deep, masculine sweet voice, lacking his heartfelt hugs, void of his gentle touch and absent the lingering kiss from his sensitive lips?

Who will take Penny for quiet walks in the forest or accompany her to college plays or music recitals? Who will attend church with her or dine in a quaint and quiet little out-of-the-way restaurant? A new life awaits Penny, one she fears she will certainly not love, but one she must accept, for Penny has many duties to perform and a lifetime's worth of many incredible memories to cherish.

Chapter 2
Meeting Penny

For as far as the eye could see, there were scenic rocky mountain peaks still covered with snow on this alluring June afternoon. Dove hiked about a mile from his blue 1963 Chevy pickup truck, using a rather worn trail that gently ascended from the warmer valley floor to blustery Bow Summit. Along the way, dainty spring flowers were majestically poking their colorful heads up from between stones and roots that covered what little soil was near the surface.

Mostly the miniature plants were Arctic asters and daisies covered with small pink, yellow, white and blue blossoms, but occasionally an area with bright red pixie cups or Arctic poppies reached for the sunlight from a tiny darkened crevice, and covered the mountainside with triumphant dazzling color. After Dove had hiked for fifteen or twenty minutes, the path grew steeper, and as he rounded a bend he encountered the most striking panoramic view he had ever seen. He saw no sign on the highway announcing, "The view of a lifetime lies ahead." Nothing in the small parking area encouraged tourists to hike a few moments to explore all that nature has to offer.

Many times, as the years passed, Dove pondered if God inspired him to make that short afternoon hike up that fabulously beautiful mountain, for passing the overlook parking stop in his pickup truck would have altered his life forever.

Looking down into the deep valley below, a peculiarly shaped lake which accumulated the summer runoff water from mighty, ancient glaciers created a blue hue like none Dove had ever seen. As he continued to circle the mountainside for an ever better view, he glimpsed a young woman peering at the stunning lake far below. She was so overwhelmed and enthralled with the scenic beauty beneath soaring mountains in the distance, she spoke aloud as if complimenting the view itself. The continual chatter of the camera shutter enumerated just how fascinated and beguiled these sights were to this enchanting female photographer.

Dove realized the young woman thrilled over her chance sighting of Peyto Lake, and she had not heard his silent, unhurried approach toward the craggy overlook. Her black Nikon camera was at the ready with a bright red carry strap slung about her neck. The viewfinder at her eye focused sharply on the legendary deep blue lake surrounded by fragrant evergreen forests and bald snow-capped mountaintops. A rich blue sky dotted with a few small puffy clouds near the horizon majestically provided contrast and framed the lake. Her army green backpack was at her feet as she rested against a fragrant fir tree that supported her balance, and provided stability for steadying and focusing the zoom lens.

The forest was silent without even a breeze as Dove stopped dead in his tracks, not wanting to disturb this delightful scene of total concentration about fifty feet ahead. He could hear the subtle click each time she pressed the shutter release, and then she searched for an even better view or perhaps a unique angle for the next photo. Dove thought, "This woman is a good

11

photographer with the patience to find the correct exposure and framing for each image captured." A Clark's Nutcracker quietly perched in a towering lodgepole pine dressed in its new spring candles, and growing on the side of the jagged mountain, reaching for the high warming sun. The large light gray bird with black wings seemed at ease in his dense surroundings, ignoring both first-time intruders who were exploring his personal grandiose mountain space.

After what seemed like several minutes Penny lowered her camera from her eye and she turned towards Dove, somewhat surprised to see anyone at such close range without hearing an approach. "I hope she knows I'm not spying on her," Dove thought, feeling his face blush red as she spoke. Dove froze, unable to move his mouth to utter a sound as she approached. Her face, without a doubt, was the most breathtaking Dove had ever seen. His eyes fixated on her loveliness, a beauty which took his breath away. Her tanned face contrasted with her radiant, perfectly aligned white teeth, and Dove's focus observed her dainty, but shapely features. She wore no makeup and had long, straight, jet black hair hanging below her neckline. Dove's lips moved, but nothing would come forth, so he blushed even more and cleared his throat. "What should I say," he thought, "how can I break the ice?"

Here, he was a twenty-four year old awestruck college graduate with a master's degree, who for the first time in his life, seemed powerless to speak. When Dove's voice finally came to life he finally blurted out, "I'm so sorry, I never meant to stare, but I have never seen such a beautiful face in my entire life!" Then, Dove nearly panicked and ran away from someone he would like to know. Dove was thoroughly embarrassed and totally at a loss for words. "She must think I'm an absolute moron," he thought.

"I'm Penny Stevens," she said, "That may be the kindest thing anyone ever said about me. I'm sorry I made you uncomfortable." Then the graceful, diminutive beauty began to walk towards Dove, and she put her tiny hand out to greet him. Her graciousness permeated Dove's inner being, and he relaxed, and instantly responded with, "Hi Penny, I'm Dove Scott," as he reached his hand toward hers. "I don't think I've ever heard Dove as a first name," Penny said, "but I think there may be some Doves that live in Warren. I don't think I've ever met any though." Dove quickly pointed out his real name was Jon, after his father; but his mother called him Dovie, "and, I guess Dove just stuck!"

She was wearing bluejeans with a white button-up blouse and a soft pink sweater. There were three buttons at the top, all buttoned except for the top. A small pink hair clip matched her sweater and restrained her hair from falling over her fabulously deep blue eyes; a shade seldom seen on a raven-haired beauty. She wore dusty, dark brown hiking boots that appeared to be well-worn and comfortable.

After such a precarious meeting, Dove found Penny to be incredibly verbose and easy to get to know. He learned she was from a small town in the northwestern part of Pennsylvania situated at the confluence of the Allegheny River and the Conewango Creek. She had recently graduated from college a few weeks earlier and was taking a short vacation prior to beginning her first professional job. Penny was going to teach third grade in her small hometown of Warren, and unbelievably, Dove was from Grove City, PA, just two hours southwest of Warren, near the Ohio border.

There they were two people from the same general area of western Pennsylvania meeting in the Canadian Rocky Mountains, thousands of miles from home. Dove was mixing vacation time with a ten day business trip to scout out a possible location for a magazine writer's conference, and then to photograph an Ukrainian Festival in Manitoba on his way home.

As they conversed, Dove turned his camera on, and started towards the location where he first saw Penny peering down the steep hillside towards the magnificent lake view. Inspired, he took multiple photos of Peyto Lake, and then asked Penny if he could take some photos of her with the wolf-head shaped lake as a backdrop. Graciously, she perched on a large boulder at the edge of the commanding overlook, and Dove found himself focused on her angelic face with a panoramic view of the lake in the background. Because of the sun's brightness, he was able to stop-down the lens, and get both Penny and Peyto Lake in sharp focus using his professional single lens reflex camera. Both subjects, Penny and Peyto Lake, contained beauty like Dove had never appreciated before and he wanted a record of both.

Life was tremendously exciting that afternoon as they explored the behemoth mountains together and began a romance Dove never thought imaginable. It was late afternoon when they returned to their vehicles and headed for Deer Lodge at Lake Louise, Alberta, where they agreed to reconnect to continue their exploration of the Canadian Rockies together.

Chapter 3
Hiking Lake Louise

D eer Lodge is the hotel next to the Chateau Lake Louise, a resort complex on the shores of exquisite Lake Louise. The Chateau is world famous and frequented regularly by the rich and famous, not to mention royalty from all continents of the world. Dove would like to have stayed at either splendid location, but he carried his sleeping gear along with his clothing, a few essential items for cooking, and his personal items in the covered bed of his small pickup truck. Still, the freedom to travel with fewer expenses was necessary as his lot in life was still under construction.

Penny, on the other hand, had rented a small room at Deer Lodge for five nights. The starkly decorated accommodation was a first level room with an unusually small square window overlooking the flowered courtyard, but without a view of either Lake Louise or the soaring cordillera in the distance, hence the hotel's most economical room. Deer Lodge was once quite a hotel in its own right but located next to the celebrated Chateau, the comparison was drastic. Gradually over the years, it became a modest alternative for travelers not wishing to spend their life's savings for their accommodation.

Dove agreed to follow Penny to Deer Lodge because he already had decided he would follow her anywhere she led, and he continued to wonder why she considered asking him along. Additionally, he was camping four or five miles from Lake Louise, so it was close. After Penny registered, Dove helped her unload her belongings from the rental car. He carried a medium sized suitcase and a garment bag into her quaint little room, and they discerned at once why the room was affordable. When they claim cozy in their ad, they mean tiny! Nevertheless, there was plenty of room for one. Besides, Penny had no intention of being in the room for anything other than sleeping. Penny had come to explore the Canadian Rockies, not live in opulence.

After depositing the suitcase on her bed and hanging the garment bag in the armoire, they walked towards picturesque Lake Louise and the marvelous lakeside chateau which was still well lit by the evening June sun. The size, location and allure of this magnificent chateau astonished the pair of explorers. Here, on the outskirts of a tiny town, not much more than a wide spot in the road, stood an incredible hotel with over five hundred rooms overlooking the world famous glacier-formed Lake Louise.

Penny said, "It's early Dove. I'd like to walk around the lake. Would you care to join me?" It was already past time for dinner, and his hunger screamed for a sandwich or more; but Dove wasn't about to end their time together by mentioning his ravenous appetite, so he answered with a nod, and with their cameras about their necks, they headed for the trail that circled the glassy smooth lake.

They passed the active canoe rental facility, taking the easy walking trail which festooned with many scenic photo-taking opportunities. Penny led the way and Dove followed a few steps behind. Where small feeder streams replenished the lake she waited for him, grasping his hand as they gingerly used stepping stones to traverse the shallow water. Soon they were holding hands all along the trail, and he found her tiny hand tightly wrapped in his when they stopped to rest on rustic wooden trailside benches.

Dove found his voice as they became acquainted, sharing life experiences during their exploration. When they crossed the lake's source at the far end of the glacier fed lake, Dove recognized darkness would be upon them within the hour, and he urged they hasten back to Deer Lodge. A yellow fingernail moon was already high in the sky, and the evening chill was well underway. Realizing his day with Penny was nearing its end, he was trepidatious he might never see her again as they devoured a snack and a soft drink from a lakeside concession on the shore of Lake Louise. As Dove walked Penny to her room, he wondered, "How can I make this sensational woman know I think she is exceptionally special?" He did not want to lose her, but he had just met her a few hours before.

Chapter 4
Remembering Their Meeting

This morning, Penny was sitting in the same chapel pew reminiscing about the day she met Dovie, high atop a beautiful mountain in the Canadian Rockies. She had resolved to quit feeling sorry for herself, and remember the forty-six magical years they had together, instead of dwelling any longer on her grief and loneliness. Every Thursday, she planned to return to the chapel to concentrate on Dovie and their fulfilling lives together.

As she sat in the beautiful gothic chapel, she thought, "I will never forget, as long as God allows me to draw a breath, how Dove approached me on the mountain overlook, and how he was tongue-tied when I spoke." Here, was a truly handsome man, in every sense of the word, awestruck by a young woman that considered herself rather ordinary. God in His goodness invoked people to have different tastes, and I could tell Dove found me attractive. When we were young adults, smaller women were more popular than the long legged model types of today. Men seemed to enjoy being a few inches taller and more athletic than their dates.

Dove was tall and muscular, with a rugged, suntanned face radiating confidence and self-discipline. His wide-set eyes were above a straight nose with small indentations made by eyeglasses; and he owned a small dimple in each cheek and brilliant teeth displayed whenever he smiled. That stupendous day, Dove wore a long sleeved, watch plaid flannel shirt with faded blue jeans and brown western boots. He prepared himself for the cooler temperatures of late spring, sporting a Pittsburgh Pirates baseball cap and a light blue jacket slung over his shoulder should the need arise.

Penny later learned the eyeglasses assisted for reading and, of course, when the sun required filtering for his piercing blue eyes. His narrow lips moved slowly when he spoke, and often displayed smiles as he listened. As their friendship grew, two of the most delightful of Dove's unique characteristics were his ability to communicate his thoughts and understand Penny's expressions correctly.

Dove stood a full head taller than Penny, with long legs that propelled him much faster than she could manage, but he was quick to recognize the span of his stride and tapered back to something decidedly suitable for her. They stopped often and caught their breath before heading onward and upward to towering heights. When Penny took his hand, she felt his lengthy fingers signal the firm grip of an athlete as he totally enclosed her small palm and tiny fingers. He squeezed gently, hinting he enjoyed holding hands. Viewing the proportions of his arms and hands, she could envision him leaping high in the air and catching a football with just one giant meat hook.

Penny knew life brings opportunities people never expect or foresee, but never in her wildest dreams did she ever contemplate meeting her soul-mate as she explored the

19

Canadian Rockies alone. Both Dove and Penny were out to hike a mountain and see what was beyond the trail's next twist. Neither had an inkling they would find a lifelong love that bright and sunny day, as they overlooked picturesque Peyto Lake. Dove had an unquestionable commitment to continue up the mountain, round one more crescent on the path, and take one more photo before calling it quits. As they hiked, Dove's stride was the embodiment of agility, and his choice of words was flawless as they ascended the trail to the mountaintop. Penny recalled her disappointment when they completed their hike and Dove escorted her back to Deer Lodge when darkness arrived. She pondered, "Will I ever see Dove again?" She hoped she would see him again, many times!

Looking back, Dove was a consistent, goal-oriented man throughout their lifetime together, always showing restraint when required, but perpetually attempting to improve over the previous result, whatever the standard. Penny was the luckiest person in the world having known and loved Dovie for forty-six years. She believed the first forty-six hours with Dove provided more pleasure than many people enjoy in a lifetime.

Penny knows her lamenting must end, and she needs to move on with her life, but still she yearns for more days with Dovie. Penny is unable to expunge his love from her mind, heart and soul, nevertheless, she will learn to subsist alone with her forty-six years of sublime memories. There will never be another Dovie!

Chapter 5
Penny in Bed

After a piping hot shower, Penny lay in her soft, warm bed with both pillows fluffed under her head, with blankets to spare. She dressed in pink and yellow shortie pajamas that reached halfway to her knees, as she sipped a cup of fragrant green tea. Before showering, Penny had unpacked her suitcase, neatly placing her folded clothes in the antique dresser beneath the small square window with the courtyard view. Flowery pink and beige wallpaper decorated the compact room, but there was plenty of space for one person. A rather large brown clock radio rested on the nightstand beside a black telephone which connected directly to the front desk.

Dove and Penny stopped at a lakeside snack shop for a quick bite to eat as they headed back toward Deer Lodge. Darkness arrived too soon, and he said goodnight with a short kiss on her cheek when he dropped Penny at her room. Penny hated to see Dove leave as he drove the pickup away from Deer Lodge into the bracing temperatures expected outdoors that night. As the wind increased and the thermometer plummeted, she worried he would be cold and uncomfortable in a sleeping bag laying on the cold, hard metal surface of the truck bed.

As Penny reclined into bed, she thought about Dove lifting her for that sweet kiss. She wondered if he forced himself past his shyness, or was he anticipating her kiss in return. She reviewed in her mind some of the stories he told her of his life, because that night sleep was not to come easily.

Dove was a Presbyterian preacher's kid, and with it came the good and the bad. He lived in a manse which was generally next door to the church, and he always felt he had to walk a tightrope to keep his father's reputation in tact. Another thing he disliked was his father relocated from city to city every six or eight years, so he constantly had to develop new companions and attend different schools with each move. Roots were an essential issue, and Dove planned to build his career where he could establish an anchored future.

Of course, he liked church and enjoyed hearing about God and the Bible; however, he believed once a week was enough for a growing boy. Dove loved his mother and father, and he fervently tried to delight them and make them proud of their only son. Although his mother wanted to birth her own child, preferably a daughter, much to her disappointment no babies arrived as she was unable to conceive until after they adopted Dove. He became the joy God sent to enrich Ron's life, and a son to carry his name forward to other generations. Surprisingly, like so many determined adults unable to conceive a child, Dove's mother, Laura, gave birth to his sister, Jennifer, before his fifth birthday, just two years after the couple adopted Dove.

He liked that his father did not have to work all day, every day, because they could hunt and fish together while most boys could only be with their dad on weekends. Additionally, his father liked baseball, basketball and football, and he encouraged Dove in every sport. Penny remembered Dove said, "Dad wasn't the best sportsman, but he always seemed to know someone able to coach me with hitting a baseball, catching a football or playing basketball. Whatever the need, dad always knew someone that could help. I thank my family every day for providing a great life for me at great inconvenience and expense to them. Few adopted children have the wonderful and caring parents God found for me."

Before, his parting kiss that night, Dove asked, "May I see you in the morning? We could have another fabulous day exploring the area." Then Penny knew Dove was someone exceptional, and looked up into his intensely blue eyes. He wrapped his long arms around Penny, lifted her off the floor and kissed her cheek. Thrilled, Penny, returned the kiss — right on the lips. Then Dove disappeared into the cold night!

Chapter 6
Cold Night in the Truck

Sleeping out under the stars can be great fun, but in deep forests with grizzly bears and who knows what, one needs to sleep with open eyes, particularly on a dark and dank night. Dove was a fearless but cautious camper when he bivouacked in an unfamiliar area. His food was carefully stored in an insulated cooler, that was locked in the truck cab to keep scents away from critters scrounging for leftovers from a campsite. Penny was in her warm, comfortable bed hours ago, but Dove curled up in an Arctic type sleeping bag designed for tundra overnights. An air mattress insulated him from the cold, hard floor of the pickup bed, but it didn't compare to a double bed in a heated private room. The crystal clear sky and high mountain elevation caused night-time temperatures to drop well below forty degrees, and the slow leak in his air mattress soon caused discomfort when his back eventually met the cold steel truck bed. Briefly, he had a hypnopompic night.

That was when the irritation, stiffness, pain and suffering started. Dove's long, muscular legs were tender from steep mountain hiking, and his irritated back ached from the steel truck bed. Dove slipped out of the warm sleeping bag three times to re-inflate the mattress. Finally, after the third time, he drifted off to sweet dreams of Penny. Dove realized the last two years he exercised less and studied more because of his advanced program at Cornell. The courses consumed too much precious time for serious hiking. Additionally, Dove finished his years of college football games and practices. Each time he awoke, Dove reflected on his gratifying day with Penny, always envisioning her allure and attractiveness. Sleep eluded Dove because his tireless mind was ablaze with her pretty face, and the whisper of her sweet voice calling in his ears. The delightful memory of that marvelous, quick kiss on the lips, sent Dove a subtle message he could not ignore. "I know Penny likes me, and tonight my heart and mind cannot rest!"

That protracted night, despite his physical discomfort, Dove realized something tremendous was imminent. He had a deep sense of joy and happiness like he never had before, and he could hardly wait for daybreak to begin a new, imaginative day with Penny. How could this little wisp of a woman charm and capture his heart, making him yearn for her, instead of falling asleep? He wondered, "Is Penny thinking about me tonight! Is there any chance she could have this same romantic feeling I have tonight, that special veiled sensation I have never known before? Could she love me too?"

Dove was truly happy when dawn broke, awakening the neighboring wildlife; and he knew the warming sun would not be far behind. Dove faced the refreshing, frigid morning temperature with joy, though his aching body was ready to find something softer. Then he thought about Penny for the first time that morning. Her image appeared in his mind with his first waking thought as he splashed cold water on his unkempt hair and suntanned face, and he felt his leg and back muscles relax and the pain dissipate.

Dove kept thinking, "Wow, I love everything about Penny. Not only is she the most beautiful woman I have ever met, she has an incredible personality, inquisitive intellect and our conversation comes naturally as we explore the rough terrain together. Her interests are my interests and her thoughts are in sync with mine. Could this woman perchance be the lady for my future?"

Penny's narration of her life's story, centered on her experiences after her birth father placed her in a small box, and left her at the back door of Doctor and Mrs. Jake Stevens' North Warren, PA home. Penny was proud of her highly respected adoptive parents, a medical doctor and his dedicated nurse-wife who found Penny tucked in a small, clean cardboard box, wrapped with only a soft, warm blanket, with a brief summary letter tucked within. Penny had memorized the letter and recited it to Dove.

April 15, 1943

Dear Dr. And Mrs. Stevens:

I am unable to care for this beautiful child though I already love her very much. Her mother died early this morning, and I am leaving her in your trust. I pray God will direct your placement, so she has a happy life. We named her Penny. Her birth date was April 10, 1943. She weighed 6 pounds and 6 ounces. Please find a home for her, one that will provide love and joy to one so small and precious.

Thank you so very much for your consideration as you place my daughter. I do love her, I just cannot care for her alone.

Penny's Father

Chapter 7
Yoho National Park

As Dove's powerful truck's engine purred and his portable gas stove warmed water for morning coffee, he opened a sack of bagels already adorned with peanut butter. He kept all his food tightly packed in a cooler within the truck cab, preventing wildlife from raiding throughout the night.

Rejuvenated from the memory of the previous day's excellent adventure, and with his stomach filled, he was ready to start another day in the enchanting Canadian Rockies, and departed the camp site heading for Deer Lodge. To his delight, Penny met him, already prepared to leave when he gently tapped on her door at 7 o'clock. Penny faced the world for another exciting day's adventure with Dove. She stepped into the hall and headed for the lobby. What's more, her hiking attire looked even more outstanding than the day before. Her blue jeans and boots looked familiar, but her soft, fragrant hair protruded into a long, braided ponytail. She wore a wine red jacket zipped up to her chin. Dove felt he should pinch himself to be sure he was fully awake and not dreaming. He cautiously poured her a cup of scalding hot coffee from his thermos, and offered her a peanut butter bagel, promising to stop for fresh, roasted coffee on the way to Emerald Lake if she wanted more.

"You're up bright and early Penny, are you ready for a day trip to Emerald Lake," he asked. "Emerald Lake, where is that Dove?" He explained it was only an hour's drive northwest from Deer Lodge, in Yoho National Park, in the easternmost part of British Columbia. Dove told her Emerald Lake's beautiful green color determined the name, unlike other regional lake's deep azure blue. He was unsure why the unique color, but he planned to find the answer.

"Well, lead the way Dove, we can head out and get another cup of hot coffee on the way," Penny announced as she started for the door. "And thanks for the bagel, Dove, I love peanut butter bagels."

Already, Dove had the sneaking suspicion he and Penny unquestionably treasured their new friendship after less than a full day together. Her voice played like soft music on his receptive ears; and her ability to communicate so easily was an endearing quality new to him. Many people study their words in route from their brain to their lips, but Penny clearly enumerated her thoughts without hesitation, not being a wordsmith.

Penny relaxed with her new friend, and felt more comfortable exploring the majestic outdoors than when she was alone. It was not because she was afraid of being out in remote country unescorted, but she could remember reading too many heinous newspaper stories of demented predators looking for a solitary young woman. Traveling the deep woods with a brawny man standing well over six feet tall and weighing nearly two hundred pounds put her mind at ease. Already she had complete trust in her traveling companion, even though she barely knew him.

Dove was a writer and photographer who had recently earned his Master of Arts Degree with a concentration in creative writing. He had completed his undergraduate work at Grove City College in Grove City, Pennsylvania and received his Master of Fine Arts degree from Cornell. Penny didn't know much about Grove City other than it was a Methodist or Presbyterian college, and it was difficult to be admitted there. She knew Cornell was a prestigious Ivy League University, having one of the top graduate schools in the nation.

The couple stopped to purchase a submarine sandwich and two Cokes for lunch, along with another cup of java for the road before arriving at their charming destination. There were not many places for food or fuel along the way, so they checked their tires and fueled Penny's rental car. Along the way, they saw a grizzly bear with two small cubs scampering across the road ahead, so Penny pulled off the road, and they watched the bears scurry towards the summit, only pausing to verify they escaped. Dove's Canon 35mm reflex camera was recording photos until the bears crossed over a ridge and slipped from view. Other than a few mule deer seen at a distance, this was their first big game sighting.

Driving Penny's rental car, they had barely finished their coffee when they entered British Columbia and Yoho National Park. The day was starting out lovely, with another high sky, but a sharp, crisp chill infused the air due to their elevation and the early hour. Although the end of June was near, snow covered most of the mountain peaks, and on the northern slopes snow reached down deep into the valleys. Of course, the black asphalt roads were all dry and safe as they absorbed heat from the bright midday sun.

Emerald Lake is difficult to characterize due to the emerald green color and the topography of the area. Just a couple of miles away is Takakkaw Falls, cascading twelve hundred feet from the top of jagged cliffs, sourcing a river and the water beneath Natural Bridge overlook. After parking the rental car, they headed to the lake and began to hike through this noticeably unique terrain that higher moisture and the lake's lower elevation affected. This combination provided selections of flora not seen around the other lakes they viewed. One bright red canoe in the distance carried a couple with fishing poles in hand while they slowly drifted across the calm, serene water. Unlike most of the lakes they were to investigate in the Canadian Rockies, the trail was somewhat difficult, especially as they circled back near the starting point. The only way to complete the circuit was to climb a steep ridge and pass through Emerald Lake Lodge and Conference Center, a delightful resort for business meetings that Dove wanted to remember.

They walked and talked with the camaraderie of a couple that had known each other for years, yet they hardly knew one another. As they hiked, they shared stories of their families, friends and their dreams for the future. This was a splendid day they enjoyed together, but it was not over — just yet!

Chapter 8
Dinner at Deer Lodge

Once again, when they headed back toward Deer Lodge, their legs were fatigued and cramping, but the triumph of having completed another physically exhausting day was thrilling for both. This pair of hikers, who didn't yet know they were a couple, discussed dinner alternatives and touched on the next day's plan, yet they verbalized nothing about the coming night. Fog drifted down into the valleys as they drove towards Deer Lodge, making it conspicuously clear that the nighttime temperatures were getting colder — much colder. Both were rather grungy and sweaty from the strenuous hiking, and they were ravenous when they arrived at the rustic old lodge.

"Let's freshen up and eat here at the lodge," Penny suggested. Penny's wardrobe didn't include anything suitable for dining at the Chateau Lake Louise, but equally crucial, they decided to avoid the costly fare. By the time Dove went to his truck and had sorted through his clothes, Penny was already in the tiny shower letting soapy water, as hot as she could stand, loosen the grime she felt all over her body. Dove waited until

Penny stepped from the bathroom modeling an oversized white terrycloth robe, provided by the lodge. He entered the small bathroom to shower while she dressed.

One fascinating fact that appealed to Dove was Penny's ability to dress for dinner swiftly, including drying and styling her hair. After his shower, Dove had gone into the quiet little lobby where he purchased a Calgary newspaper to catch up on world events of the past few days. As he was glancing through the sports pages, he was startled when Penny announced, "I'm ready," as she entered the lobby.

She was wearing beige slacks with a dark blue satin blouse. Penny had a delicate gold cross suspended from her neck on a short, fine chained, gold necklace. She wore small gold button-like earrings, and a matching ring on her pinky finger. Her brown flats with open toes and ankle straps appeared new, and covered her flesh colored nylons. Looking up from his chair, Dove noticed the striking woman he was beginning to love, and he invited, "Let's head to the restaurant and check the menu, Penny." He felt proud as they walked hand-in-hand through the lobby and into the warm, comfortable restaurant, each table displaying a flickering candle.

It was apparent her wardrobe was stylish and nearly new; but he questioned, "how could anyone be so lovely wearing simple, casual clothes?" As Dove stood he felt taller, more important and delighted, because Penny was his dinner date. Penny's flowing ebony hair was styled differently once again, but her eyes sparkled with the same fabulous deep blue hue, complimenting her stunning blouse. For the first time, he observed she had applied a small amount of pinkish lipstick and possibly a touch of blush and eyeliner. "Is that a delicate scent of perfume?" he wondered. Dove loved the slight aroma she presented.

Penny sat in subdued lighting, watching Dove glance over the tempting menu. Could this man be more than just a casual acquaintance of two days? She noticed his neck was thick, and his upper body muscular, and narrowed down to his waist. He obviously worked out, and she fantasized he was probably a sports star in college. She thought it was no surprise when he confessed he was a wide receiver at Grove City College. When she saw the size of the hands holding his utensils, she had no doubt. Dove had a full head of naturally wavy short, dark brown hair, the kind that always looked newly styled. His eyes sparkled from the dim candlelight, and reflected the flame as Penny observed him from across the table. Dove was clean shaven and dressed in neatly pressed khaki slacks with a blue dress shirt, unbuttoned at the top, covered by a navy crew neck sweater. His brown loafers were newly shined, and he wore no jewelry. Penny thought Dove looked like an Ivy Leaguer as he sipped on his water.

They both ordered succulent rainbow trout with all the fixings, including sweet potato fries, green beans sprinkled with bacon bits, and soft dinner rolls. They even shared a dessert made with a special basil flavored ice cream over lemon cake. Before the meal was concluded, their conversation had become very personal with questions of their past lives, and what they planned for their futures. Dove explained he was raised by his family's pastor and his wife after his mother died of tuberculosis, and his father was killed during World War Two. Dove's grandmother, his only other relative, passed away a few days after she received the news of her son's death. Dove joked that being a Presbyterian PK, preacher's kid, was probably the reason he was admitted to Grove City College, as acceptance was difficult. He related experiences of his early years in Franklin, Butler, New Castle, Erie and finally Grove City, Pennsylvania. His father was now the dean of the college chapel, along with duties teaching New Testament Literature to freshman. At the meal's conclusion, over a second cup of decaf, they looked down, and realized they were holding hands.

The heavy steel door in the lobby was caught by continuous gusts of wind, forcing it open part-way before repeatedly slamming closed. The rustling tree limbs joined the creaking of large plate glass windows providing a symphony of Mother Nature's stormy fury as they departed the restaurant, and walked through the empty lobby. Returning down the hallway towards her room, Penny urged, "Dove, you can't go out in these elements. It's unsafe for you to sleep outside in the truck tonight."

Of course, Dove wasn't excited about the prospects of a cold, windy night in the truck with an air mattress that leaked, but he really had nowhere else to go, and the lodge was fully occupied. "Oh, I'll be all right, and besides, this may die down in an hour or two. I'll survive the night!"

"Well, let's sit and talk some before you make a decision you may regret, Dove. There's another thing I want to talk with you about, anyway. I know this sounds vacuous, after knowing you for only two days, but I think, … I, … well, I think I may have already fallen in love with you." Dove could have toppled off the three legged dressing table stool he was sitting, for he had genuinely never been in love. Oh, there were a few girls in his life, but they were only acquaintances. He had never been serious about anyone. He looked at her again, re-living the memory of when they first met, unable to speak; not knowing what to say or how to speak his thoughts.

She could tell he was at a loss for words, so she rose from the only chair in the room and walked over to Dove. She took his hands in hers, urged him from the stool, and as tears streamed down her cheeks she said, "May I at least have one small kiss before you tell me that you don't love me?"

Dove stood in front of her, dwarfing her tiny figure with his athletic body. He reached for a Kleenex on the dresser and blotted away her streaming tears. Then Dove effortlessly lifted her until their eyes met, their lips touched, and their hearts became one. Penny threw her arms around Dove's neck and squeezed for all she was worth. Dove's vocal cords constricted as he whispered, "Penny, I wasn't signaling I don't love you, I was just shocked and elated beyond words that someone as wonderful, smart and beautiful as you would ever say they loved me. Yes, I love you, more than I can possibly say. You are like a dream that continues to improve and excite, minute after minute."

Penny was still clinging to Dove as he continued holding her in his strong arms when she blurted out, "Dove, I want you to stay with me — tonight and every night, and I want you to love me gently. Please don't laugh at me when I say this, but I'm a little scared. You see, I've never loved a man before." Penny thought it was like she assayed Dove's soul and found pure gold.

He set her down, and again he was at a loss for words. Previously, Dove had agonized that Penny would find him unacceptable, and now his dream was about to be realized. Finally, he ventured, "I don't want you to think I'm a man with great experience, Penny. We're going to have to learn how to love together." Their passion was intense that night, and they knew their search for love was finished as they forgot loneliness and found a lifetime of happiness.

Chapter 9
Canadian Marriage

Their first morning together after such an exciting and eventful night, they remained in the arms of Morpheus until nearly 8 o'clock before considering giving up the comfy bed. Dove made a monumental decision, and made a suggestion that seemed surreal, even to him, "Penny, let's get married today, right here in Canada. We can telephone our parents and promise them that we will come home and reaffirm our vows in church. As a matter of fact, I know dad will want to officiate the marriage ceremony at Grove City College, if that would be agreeable to you and your parents." Dove expected Penny to be shocked and recite hundreds of reasons why he was certifiable, but she only asked, "Will they marry us in Canada," then she paused and said, "today Dove — are you sure?"

Penny called the front desk to ask about marriage licenses and waiting periods; and she happily learned if they were over eighteen years of age, all that was required was the marriage license fee and verifiable identification such as a passport or driver's license. Later that afternoon, they drove to Banff and found a family owned jewelry store located in a small building on the main drag. The saleslady offered some tasteful, but affordable classic gold wedding bands that fit their fingers without adjustment. The jeweler-owner rang up the sale, and provided two perfect wedding gifts as he delicately engraved each band with the wedding date, their initials and with love while they waited. Excited with the wedding bands and the precious gift, Penny and Dove immediately headed for the Marriage Commissioner's office where they were pronounced husband and wife at four o'clock on Monday, June 21, 1965, the longest day of the year. The newlyweds proceeded to telephone their parents and best friends, telling every person of their great joy and deep love. Dove felt like the happiest and luckiest man who ever lived, and Penny was overjoyed being married to Dove, the handsome man she would love forever.

They were so proud of their embossed marriage certificate with all the required signatures, including Martin Roller, Marriage Commissioner, Lake Louise, Alberta, attesting Jon Scott and Penny Stevens were united in marriage on June 21, 1965. Their happiness was only beginning as they loved and talked into the wee hours of the morning. They laughed about their "first" honeymoon, and discussed where they would go for their second honeymoon in August, after the formal chapel wedding. When Penny and Dove arrived back at the lodge, a beautiful wedding card, a dozen long stemmed red roses and a chilled bottle of champagne were on the nightstand. A second white terrycloth bathrobe was on the bed with a dining certificate for two. Everything was compliments of the Deer Lodge staff.

That night, over another candlelight dinner, they continuously admired the shiny gold bands on their fingers, proudly knowing their significance. Dove said, "This circle of gold has no beginning and has no end. Your gold band represents that my love for you and our marriage will be like a circle with no beginning and no end. I make that commitment to you right now, and forever." Dove had heard his father use those lines in several marriages he had attended over the years, and he knew he wanted Penny to understand his commitment and desire to be united forever.

Tears were streaming down Penny's face, and she nearly sobbed, "That's the second time your words have touched me deeply. I promise you Dove that I will always love and honor you and be your best friend as long as I live, so help me God." The church wedding was planned for the first Saturday in August at the Grove City College Harbison Chapel. Dove's father would officiate, and Dr. Stevens would give the bride away.

Chapter 10
Penny's Most Joyful Days

A nother week has passed since Dovie passed. Penny felt fortunate to be able to come to campus every Thursday, if only for a few hours to dwell on her life's unwritten story. The students, with their vigor and eternal optimism, comforted and renewed Penny with each visit. Her seemingly endless days are bustling with long-time friends and carrying on Dove's and her mission here in Grove City, but her nights are empty and meaningless. Some other day Penny will think about their foundation for unwed mothers, but not today. She only wants to remember her first few days with Dovie and the passionate happiness that never ended or even dimmed once he entered into her life.

First impressions always were paramount when Penny selected friends. Sometimes she remembers their chance encounter when they met on that overlook as she photographed Peyto Lake. Dove didn't "come on" to her as the young people say today. He patiently waited for Penny to conclude photographing the scenery before he approached the spectacular view below. Penny could clearly observe he was blushing when she spoke to him, and she knew he was searching for a pleasant response. During her life, Penny dreamed about his unique first sentence, so frequently the words were always on the tip of her tongue. Even now, after all these years, she still hears the echo of his pleasant voice saying, "I'm so sorry, I didn't mean to stare, but I have never seen such a beautiful face in my entire life!" That line wouldn't have resonated had someone else spoken the words to Penny, for she clearly would have seen through a phony. Many years later, Dove created a heroic character who used those exact words in one of his outstanding novels, *Intense Love*. They were both rather private people, never the life of anyone's party except in their private affairs. They were not naïve, but they weren't exactly worldly either.

It was 1960 before Enovid (the first birth control pill) was approved by the Federal Drug Administration, when American society frowned on babies being born out of wedlock. Families often endured the torment of their children's premarital behavior, caught in the trap of either supporting and loving, or denying and disowning. Many times those young mothers-to-be were sent away for a year of "private study," rather than face the savage consequences with their extended families and former friends. Few parents had the grace to forgive a wayward daughter, let alone forget her life-altering misdeed. Too often, young women feeling alone and unloved suffered blotched abortions, often leading to horrible and obviously unnecessary deaths, rather than face their parents' wrath and friends' abandonment.

Of course, there were other methods of birth control, but they were not used by females, and they were undependable. Abstinence and/or the unreliable rhythm method were the techniques of choice for unmarried teenaged females to avoid pregnancy, not to mention a reputation in the 1960s.

Neither Dovie or Penny had ever engaged in sexual intercourse until the second day they were together in the Canadian Rockies. Looking back, Penny knows their actions sound ghastly, but she was so enraptured with Dove that she never even considered the repercussions when they spent their first night together; and although they were married the following afternoon, there were no promises that night. Dove could easily have left Penny the next day, never to see her again, but they both were smitten by cupid's honed arrow of love. Total attraction for the other captured their untested hearts, and they lost total self-control in a state of passionate first love. As Penny sits in the chapel today, there is no doubt that they would consummate their love again in the same manner, and rejoice for pleasure and closeness Dove and she enjoyed that night and subsequently for so many consecrated years.

The intense joy of being loved by Dovie was the most exciting experience Penny ever encountered, even until this very day. There was total abandonment to everything they had ever planned. Penny fully expected to remain chaste until her wedding night, but she lost all control that night of impassioned bliss, and she never regretted one minute that she had exchanged the course she planned for her life for immediate gratification. Penny was in Love.

Penny knew that very night, one day she would become Mrs. Jon Scott, but she never envisioned or hoped for it to occur the very next day, the third day of their ardent life together. It was the supreme decision, though it was the quickest consequential decision Penny ever made. They were made to be united, and after one night together, both recognized they had found true love and soul mates for life's journey.

Her heart still leaps when she recalls how Dove lifted her off the floor, with her feet dangling in space until their lips pressed together and they stared into the depths of each other's souls. Their love was consuming and passionate, and Penny rejoices every time she recalls the pleasant smile of his face, the strong touch of his massive hand, the melody and rhythm of his deep, soft words, or even his masculine fingers running through her raven black hair when she was a younger woman.

Without Dovie, Penny's life can never be the same, but her glorious memories will last forever.

Chapter 11
End of Lake Louise Vacation

The fabulous week, in Banff National Park, came to an end too soon for Penny and Dove. They resolved to stay together as long as possible until Penny's flight departed Calgary for Chicago, and then on to Buffalo where her mother would meet her at the airport. She returned her rental car and was preparing to check her bags when Dove asked, "Is there some reason you need to get home this week?" She thought for a minute about her plans and said, "No, not really, what are you thinking, Dove?"

"Perhaps I didn't tell you this, but I need to attend the Canadian National Ukrainian Festival for three days beginning next Friday, but first I plan to go up to Jasper to see and photograph Maligne Lake, one of Canada's most photographed and well known sites. Additionally, I'm checking a resort as a possible location for a magazine writer's conference next summer. After finishing up in Jasper, I plan to drive to Dauphin, Manitoba on Thursday to prepare for the festivities; then I'm heading back to Pennsylvania when the celebration concludes on Sunday." His mind was whirling as he thought of some additional enticements which might draw her attention and persuade Penny to stay and return home with him after the festival.

Penny wasn't too sure about being delayed another ten days, but when Dove said, "I want to meet your family, and additionally, your hometown of Warren has piqued my interest." She claimed she'd be right back, as she departed to cancel her flights; but Penny was delayed, and Dove started to fret. "Was I losing her already?" More considerate than Dove may have been, she called her mother to tell her that she would not be returning as planned. At the same time, Penny shared more details about Dove, the love of her young life, and updated her plans to extend their honeymoon days together.

By the time Penny returned, both were excited to have more time together to get to know each other even better as they continued honeymooning in the Canadian Rockies. As they drove north towards Jasper, Dove thought about the cottage-suite his company had booked at the Fairmont Jasper Park Lodge. He contacted the company's travel agent that made the reservations, only to learn the resort complex was one of Canada's finest. She confirmed his cabin suite would accommodate both he and Penny, and would not be an issue at the lodge. The reservationist said, "You're really going to like your suite."

Along the way, they stopped at the giant Columbia Ice Fields where they could see the ancient glacier with snow covered mountains in every direction. They stopped to take more photos, so they could share their honeymoon with friends and relatives, and begin their family photo album for when they were old and gray. They passed the Bow River to photograph the raging river with its incredibly icy blue water as it cascaded down to the valley below, creating an ever deeper gorge through solid rock. They saw elk on three occasions and one lone moose just before they entered the village of Jasper.

Penny and Dove drove through the small town of Jasper and followed their map across another charging river which wound along a narrow back road past equestrian stables, until they saw the exquisite Fairmont Jasper Lodge Resort where Dove was registered. The complex contained restaurants and gift shops and the resort was equipped with outdoor and indoor swimming pools plus a world famous golf course in the distance. A large sign advised, "Reservations Required," as they peeked into the main dining room which overlooked Lac Beauvert, as blue as any they had seen. Along the lakefront were many cottage hotel suites, some having multiple tenants, but theirs was a single unit about one hundred yards from the predominant lodge and registration lobby. Their pristine cottage was situated thirty yards from the shoreline and a short walk to the main lodge. A beautiful paved walking path meandered along the tree shaded waterfront in both directions, for as far as the eye could see. They noticed there were three tiers of cottages and were told the units beginning with 1 were in the first row.

Penny was aglow with excitement as they wound their way down to Suite 131, located on the waterfront with a glorious view of the entire lake. Small viewing docks with redwood lawn furniture were built along the shore, offering guests a serene location to read a book or watch the wildlife. Sometimes children were seen fishing from the docks, and occasionally an excited youngster would hook a trout or walleye. Canoes, kayaks and a few other manually powered boats dotted the lake, but motors were forbidden. Parking was scarce, but Dove found a spot adjacent to the cottage enabling them to carry their luggage easily.

When Dove opened the door, three large flower arrangements were inside with messages. One message read, "Congratulations on your marriage! We want you to have a great stay. Check the refrigerator." The message was signed,

"Your Writer Friends." Two other bouquets were from their parents with warm wishes for love and happiness. Inside the suite was a large living room with a TV, sofa, a couple of chairs with floor lamps, and all the necessities including a small refrigerator with a magnum of French champagne. The bedroom was huge with a king sized bed, TV, armoire, two end tables and a large walk-in closet at the far end of the room. The bathroom was spectacular with a shower large enough for a basketball team. Dove quipped, "Life is good!"

They dropped their baggage on the floor and Penny was in Dove's arms immediately, thanking him for this extended vacation of sorts. Once again, Penny wondered at her good fortune as her eyes danced, and she tugged Dove towards the comfortable, oversized bed where the couple playfully began to wrestle. It would take more than a 105 pound, five foot four inch woman to overpower Dove, but he toyed with her for several minutes before pinning her shoulders to the mattress. It was obvious Dove had coined a new phrase. "Love is good," he said as their lips met and they rejoiced in their passion of desire.

Dove was using a digital recorder on the cottage porch, dictating his fresh thoughts about the resort when Penny emerged from the shower. She was surprised at the detail as he described each room in the cottage facility, including the porch and the view of the lovely serene lake. His vocabulary wasn't stilted, but he used incredibly descriptive words as he dictated his impressions. It was immediately clear his ideas were organized and dictated sequentially to be used later. Much of his taped record could be put to paper without alteration.

They walked around the manicured campus, taking photos of various sized cottages, views, swimming pools, restaurants and the lobby area, so Dove could recall as much detail as possible for his presentation in three weeks. The resort complex included the impressive Fairmont Jasper Park Lodge Golf Course, which showcased challenging greens overlooking the tranquil lake with spectacular mountain backgrounds, as golfers tested their skill against the premier course in the Canadian Rockies. Photos on display proved the course appealed to the rich and famous as they browsed scenes with Bing Crosby, Marilyn Monroe, Queen Elizabeth and many others decorating the walls.

Dove had an expense account as he was expected to verify the quality of the hotel food as well as entertainment available in Jasper. He joked, "Penny, I know it's a tough job, but someone has to review this place and all its amenities!" They decided on dinner in Jasper as Penny did not have suitable clothes for the lodge, however, before dinner they walked past the main lodge restaurant to smell the delightful aromas that emanated from the kitchen into the lobby, and they noted the attire being worn in the restaurant. Shopping was in order before tomorrow night, because they had a duty to perform!

They selected a busy downtown restaurant, Karouzo's Steakhouse, which charmingly featured a violinist and vocalist who serenaded each table with enchanting love songs. Their first Jasper meal and the selections they chose were superior. Over a glass of chilled champagne, they toasted their love and friendship as they listened to the musicians parading from table to table. Many favorite authentic Greek dishes were available, along with Italian and Canadian fare. From the Greek menu, Dove and Penny chose a delicious Greek salad before her pastitsio and his moussaka dinners. Dove could report the selection was outstanding with Canadian steaks, Italian pastas and many Greek specialties. Best of all was the baklava pastry they shared over a cup of decaf before returning to the Fairmont Jasper Lodge to check on nightlife at the lodge.

Chapter 12
Jasper Fairmount Lodge

Penny needed some appropriate clothes for dinner. Inside the city limits, they were amazed to see many onlookers viewing an elk herd with huge antlers grazing in a meadow. At a nearby stream, three fishermen attempted to provide their evening meal as they tested their skill with fly rods.

Penny was not a woman particularly fond of shopping, but she managed to select a three piece navy blue outfit and a pair of matching heels that would enable her to arrange the ensemble into three different combinations. When she modeled the deep blue suit, Dove thought her eyes intensified from the hue and amplified their beauty. Because Dove had prepared for his sojourn to Jasper and a few evenings dining in fine restaurants, he packed appropriate attire and did not require additional formal wear.

The gray sky gave way to bright sunshine after lunch, creating an exciting opportunity to explore the walking trails and the golf course that afternoon. Golf was a new experience for Penny, but she was athletically inclined and carded sixty-three strokes when they tallied their score after nine holes. That was a pretty respectable round for a first-timer, and Dove did not challenge any course records either! Penny always claimed Dove blamed the rented golf clubs for his forty-two. Lounging around together provided another opportunity for the couple to learn more of each other and their pasts. There would be other days to explore Maligne Lake and generate some stunning images for framing.

That evening they dined in the main dining room of the famous lodge. Their reserved table was located against the massive glass windows overlooking the lake, and even though it was 8:30 when they arrived, the sun brightly lit their view due to northern latitude of Jasper and the late June date. A vase of freshly picked Arctic flowers of various colors and types decorated their Chippendale table. Large pewter chargers supported Wedgwood dinner plates accompanied by ornate silverware, with Waterford crystal water and wine goblets on each side. The table setting was exquisite.

As the sun descended in the majestic evening sky, they looked over the extensive wine list, and ordered a glass of modestly priced Bordeaux as they watched several large fish feeding in the lake. They were not overly fond of the wine, but they say one needs to develop a taste for alcohol.

Dinner was a delight, with continuous white gloved obsequious waiters and bus boys serving food fit for a king. Penny ordered rack of lamb with smashed potatoes and snap peas. The main course was preceded by a robust seafood bisque with shaved potatoes and bacon swimming in the pale, thick soup, sprinkled on the surface with paprika and parsley to add color. Dove had the splendid bisque along with a Caesar salad before his main course of lean, thick, slightly pink elk steak with a baked potato and creamed carrots.

The dessert list was inspiring; however, they rebuffed dessert and opted for decaffeinated coffee while watching the sun set over the peaceful lake. Before leaving the table, Dove took out his tiny tape recorder to chronicle the night's events. Again, the detail he dictated astonished Penny as he reviewed the meal, the service, the décor, and the picturesque view of the lake. They finished dinner at 10:40 PM, and the sun was just setting in the western sky as they returned to their cottage on the lakefront.

That night they stayed on the cottage porch for over an hour continuing to learn more about one another. Dove found there was nothing he didn't want to know about Penny and her family. Tomorrow they would drive to Maligne Lake to photograph a particularly popular site, visited by top photographers worldwide. The weather called for mostly clear skies with widely scattered clouds in the afternoon. Dove always found clouds added detail, depth and color saturation to his images. He loaded a fresh roll of Kodachrome Film into his Canon camera, then, hand-in-hand, he led her to the honeymoon bed, two lovers ending a perfect day in each other's arms. Dove was thinking of grabbing his dictation machine to record his feelings of love towards Penny, but his thoughts were indescribable that night as he lifted his Sleeping Beauty into their comfortable bed. Dove had additional reasons to live; he had someone to love, someone to hold close, and a new feeling of pride and satisfaction that would last forever. Dove's life was changed, changed for the better!

Chapter 13
Maligne Lake

The new day was beautiful! They woke early when the first light bent around the colorful red drapes, and harlequin ducks and coots noisily spread the word it was time to behold the new day. After the hearty meal consumed the night before, they decided to forgo breakfast and have a snack after they arrived at Maligne Lake. Of course, coffee was convenient at the lodge, so they started there before leaving the resort.

All along the highway they saw wildlife, more than seen during expeditions on previous days. Elk were particularly abundant, and both were surprised the elk had such heavy, massive racks so early in the year. Penny and Dove were accustomed to white-tailed deer in Pennsylvania, and they had no antlers in June, or if they did, they were small and in velvet.

Maligne is another of those lakes with cerulean water dependent on the melting of glaciers. Boat tours are contractible after June 1, to access the most picturesque and imaged area of the scenic lake; however, often ice prevents opening the lake until late in the month. Their arrival was not until shortly before noon, mainly because of the various sites and wildlife to see and photograph along the narrow roads making their way through the deep forests and splendid water sites. Penny had loaded her camera with Kodacolor film, so she could easily make color prints for her friends, but Dove was interested in color slides for his presentation to his employer.

They had eaten a gourmet Caesar salad with half a chicken salad sandwich for lunch at the popular Maligne Lake restaurant overlooking the picturesque waterfront, before they climbed aboard a tour boat around 1:30PM, and promptly headed for the view seen round the world. The small, proud grove of evergreen trees on tiny Spirit Island provided a photo with deep snow covering mountaintops from every direction. As they cruised down the lake, their guide took them close to shore where they saw a grizzly bear with two cubs. Another location presented several elk in full regal splendor, while a third site offered a brown bear and one cub fishing for dinner.

After Penny and Dove had arrived at Spirit Island, a kind gentleman took some photos of the newlyweds using their cameras because they wanted to display the magical scene in their home, not that they had a home yet. They saw mountain goats and sheep part-way up the surrounding cliffs which protruded in strange formations, displaying their winter blanket of snow and ice. Many of the peaks remain snow-covered year round, but the snow was still deep and white now, while later in the year the image changes from the clean, white snow of June to one less attractive.

Too soon the boat ride was concluded, but there were other exciting activities to pursue now. There was a canoe rental station at the head of the lake, along with vendors who combined white water rafting with boat trips on the lake. They settled for an hour canoe rental for exercise and exploration on their own while peering into the depths of crystal clear water, looking for fish. Penny loved the sights as they paddled into little coves, and both photographed beautiful shore birds of unknown species to them.

Dove continued to record his thoughts on his tiny hand held recorder, adding his ideas of activities the management team would enjoy while in Jasper. There was no doubt Dove's recommendation would be positive as they investigated the area for unique opportunities. Too bad their time in Jasper was coming to a close as they had only scratched the surface of Jasper National Park, Canada's most northerly National Park.

Returning to Jasper, they passed Medicine Lake, an anomaly of nature, which by the end of summer would be dry. The water in this lake disappears into the earth, much like water in a bathtub. It has never been fully determined where the water resurfaces though researchers have dyed the water and then searched for colored water elsewhere.

Penny and Dove were both tired and hungry by the time they returned to Jasper so finding a quaint little pizzeria was a timely discovery before winding back to the lodge. Both sat out on the porch and drifted off to sleep before the sun retired for the day.

Chapter 14
Ukrainian Festival

They rose early and had a sumptuous breakfast of hickory smoked bacon and eggs at the lodge before they packed the truck and headed for Dauphin, Manitoba. Dove gave a cursory look at the tattered map and realized the trek would take more than one day's drive. Penny settled into the co-pilot's seat as he started northeast towards Edmonton, Canada's sixth largest city, half-way to Saskatoon, Saskatchewan, where Dove planned to stay the first night. Heading out, they soon left the mountain region and entered the northern great plains where wheat was growing like corn in Nebraska. Every farm seemed to be manicured as they drove the two lane highway to Canada's National Ukrainian Festival.

As they were driving along, Dove started talking about a sermon his father gave some years ago that still resonated with him. He said, "I don't recall many of his sermons, but this one strikes home now that I've met and fallen in love with you." Dad said, "To be successful in life, one needs to have something to do, someone to love and something to look forward to every day." Dove claimed he always had plenty to do and many objectives to look towards as he made his mark in the literary world, and leaving a legacy of helping others. He continued, "Until I met you, I never really loved." Dove was able to touch Penny's heart when he spoke, and he helped her understand some of the most salient issues in life.

Penny questioned, with neither of them having a previous love, how such an overpowering attraction for one another blossomed in just a matter of hours. "Dove, how could we fall so helplessly in love in two short days, and consummate a love affair when were so inexperienced? That's plagued my mind, and I just don't understand this joint impulsiveness, Dove."

"Penny, I wish I knew the answer to that question, but I noticed something special about you with my first glance. I believe it was more than your physical beauty, for it was apparent you enjoy the same hearty outdoors activities as I pursue. I also admire your willingness to independently vacation in the Canadian Rockies, exploring alone when perhaps you were unable to find a group or someone special to make this trip with you." He explained, "The longer we hiked and talked, the more I was impressed with your determination and success as you completed college and garnered your first position. I also admire how you knew exactly what you planned to do with your life from a career point of view. You have a plan, a fabulous plan, and I will support you as you reach for your goals."

Then Dove explained there was something about her face and long coal black hair and even the modest way she dressed that excited him. "You are the image I created in my mind long ago, which has never materialized in person, until the splendid day we met." Poor Penny was struggling to maintain her composure and swiftly searched her purse for a tissue to dry her lovely deep blue eyes.

"Penny, now that I've confessed, tell me what appealed to you." Penny thought for a moment before she answered, "I'm not sure what caused the sudden attraction. I don't believe it is your physical appearance, but certainly that's a big plus. Probably the strongest attraction is your ability to listen and respond with words that linger. It is obvious you are a gentle man, one with deep feelings and concern for others." Penny went on and explained that Dove's feelings and beliefs permeated his words and made her realize he was someone extraordinarily distinctive, a man she wanted to get to know better — much better! Dove entered her heart with his words.

They stopped for a quick lunch in Edmonton, then kept on trucking across the flat farmland with barely a pit stop or two along the way. They arrived in Saskatoon about 5:30PM, grabbed dinner and then Dove retrieved his tape recorder from the truck and started to dictate. His memory was phenomenal as he provided vivid, descriptive words of their long but enjoyable trip, recalling everything from windmills to game birds they passed. The next morning they headed out for a six hour drive to Dauphin and discovered the terrain was much the same as the day before, generally flat farmland.

The little town was already full of festival participants and gleeful music by the time they arrived. Hotels were sold out, restaurants were packed and the streets were filled with people from every province and several nearby states. Most people were wearing Ukrainian garb. Small bands were on every street corner with dancers in the streets. Delicious food, including potato dumplings, cabbage borscht, stuffed cabbage rolls, deep-fried straw potatoes, chicken Kiev and poppy seed cake were available on the street.

After checking into their motel room, they walked the streets sampling the many distinctive dishes rather than seeking a formal restaurant. On Saturday, they attended the dance competitions and listened to music reminiscent of the old country. The women dancers performed in colorful tunic costumes with white aprons and beautifully embroidered white blouses with red leather boots. Many had coral necklaces and a headband with flowers and ribbons that draped down their backs as they danced.

The men wore baggy trousers with either white or black shirts with decorative stitching around the neck and down the front. Some wore vests as well, and the vests also were embroidered. Their boots were either black or white, usually matching the sash they wore around their waist.

Before the day was finished, they had realized the Ukrainians savored and protected their heritage with festivals all over Canada and the United States. These people were obviously proud to be of Ukrainian decent, and it was apparent they loved to dance, cook and display their beautiful hand-made clothing, especially the embroidered blouses nearly everyone wore.

On Sunday morning, they packed the truck and headed for Warren, PA where Dove would meet Penny's parents. Dove looked at the map and declared it would take three days of driving about eight hours each, before they would reach Warren. Penny was eager to show her new catch to her parents, and she suggested they drive a little farther on the first two days, so they could be home early on Tuesday. When they were ready to vacate the motel, Dove asked Penny to drive for the first time. He wanted to record his recollections from the festival while details were still fresh in his mind.

Their first honeymoon had been everything either could have ever expected, and they knew someday they would return to each place they had visited in Canada. They also knew Peyto Lake would be the first place revisited, because that body of water would provide the memory of a lifetime. They planned to celebrate their union with each visit.

Chapter 15
Going Home to Warren

Driving across the Canadian prairies on their way to Warren, Dove and Penny had many hours to reveal more about themselves. Without question, both were in love with life, including the lives they had been so fortunate to have lived with quality adoptive and loving families. Now they were excited about the life which lay ahead, as they rolled past miles and miles of wheat fields, lakes and small towns.

Dove told Penny about his father and his unwavering desire to see his son attend his alma mater. "He wanted me to follow in his footsteps and attend Grove City College. Dad never missed the opportunity to share his reasons why I should apply there, and get an education that was more conservative than most any other college. I don't recall him mentioning the cost factor, which was probably not a major issue as he pressed for his alma mater, but GCC tuition was very reasonable. My father had one goal that stood far above all others, and it was for me to lead a happy Christian life with a Christian woman."

"Dad would tell me, about GCC being a small college with a great reputation where many young men meet and marry their lifetime partners." The pastor related how he met his wife, Laura, at Grove City College and the overall quality of students and faculty. Year after year, Ron took his son to football, basketball, and concerts at the college, hoping to instill his love for the college to his son. Then he would boast of the many top corporate executives and government officials who were alumni from Grove City College.

Dove told Penny about his high school and college life, and his plans for more education. "Graduating from Erie East High School was a thrill for me, as I was valedictorian of the class of 1959." Dove admitted he worked hard to achieve this goal, but his private math tutor made the difference. "Some courses like English, music and literature came naturally for me, as did sports, Latin, French, science and history. Math was supremely difficult; however, I toiled many long hours in preparation for every test. Surprisingly," he said, "I felt remorse in some ways, because I received help that salutatorian, Becky Sanders, was unable to afford." Deep inside, Dove believed she was more deserving than he to be valedictorian.

When Dove started at GCC, his father was pastor of a large Presbyterian church in Erie, PA, and he expected that would be his final church. "Mom and dad were elated when he was called to be the Dean of the Chapel and teach New Testament Literature at Grove City College when Dove was a junior there. Dad loved the college, and getting that call was the highlight of his career," according to Dove, "he just could not believe he was offered this consequential and most significant position, his lifelong dream."

Dove admitted, "It is likely I would have pursued my education at another college, but I did not want to disappoint my father, and I knew GCC was a great, but small Christian college that produced many brilliant graduates. Certainly, I wasn't thinking about marriage, but I reasoned there would be many young ladies from Christian homes that could make a good match. Still, I worried I would be too restricted from developing my own beliefs and standards for my life." Then, as an afterthought, Dove said, "On the other hand, Grove City College offered me the opportunity to play varsity football where larger schools had better talent, and importantly, I met my best friend on the Wolverine football team."

"I fell in love with the students, the courses, the professors, and the campus, but I never found the right woman to take my heart. Realistically, I was involved with football, basketball, debate club and a mission trip every year, in addition to my studies, so the girl would have to wait. I was a class officer during my sophomore and junior years, and President of the Student Body during my senior year. In a word, I was too busy." Dove's many sports based achievements seemed to bother him because he knew being a football player was instrumental in winning the elections. He subconsciously felt others were more deserving.

"Although dad wanted me to study for the ministry, that was not my goal, partly because of the constant moving from church to church, and living under a microscope. I already had experience in both areas, and I knew preaching was not my calling. Also, I was afraid I would suffer from burn-out, like so many preachers, doing the same thing week after week."

"Grove City College filled my every need. I like to think I am an open-minded person, one who can listen to multiple points of view, consider the advantages and disadvantages of each, and then select the perspective that makes sense to me. I am not a dogmatic individual, and I understand wise people don't always agree, but I found the professors at Grove City College flexible and understanding of other viewpoints." Dove continued, "With very few exceptions, I found my courses were outstanding, and they prepared me for my chosen career in creative writing. He talked about his favorite professor, Dr. Adams' and how he joked, "I am so narrow-minded my ears touch." Penny laughed and quipped, "Did he really say that?"

"I assure you that he did say that, and you can believe the man was a conservative thinker, but open-minded, and always willing to listen to new ideas; and he was very generous with his time, as well. His opinions were valued by presidents as he served on three committees that reported their findings to the President of the United States. He graded more on the student's thought process than whether the student's conclusion agreed with his interpretation."

The football team's greatest year was 1962 when Dove was a junior. Their record of 11-1 still stands as the Wolverine's best ever. Their team quarterback, Bobby Morris, could run the option play and make accurate throws consistently. The team had many players excelling in their positions, but Dove knew Bobby was exceptional, and the primary reason for their outstanding record. Dove said, "I played tight-end where I generally provided blocking for the running game. Occasionally, because my size and strength allowed me to add yardage after the catch, I was Bobby's primary target on short passes over the middle. For most plays, however, I was a blocker." The Wolverines hoped to be undefeated the following year but Bobby was injured in the first game of the 1963 campaign, dashing their hopes for an undefeated season.

Dove spoke of Bobby Morris. Bobby was the Wolverine's star, who was not only out for the season, but finished with football for the rest of his life. He received a crushing blow to his helmet, separating him from his head gear, and then he was accidentally kicked behind his left ear as he fell to the ground. Bobby lay unconscious in the University of Pittsburgh Medical

Center for nearly three weeks before opening his eyes, and he was unable to return to GCC until the following year. He remained immobilized in the hospital for nearly four months to prevent further injury to his damaged skull and neck. As he drove across Canada, Dovie choked a little as he told the story about his best friend. "Bobby was my friend, my best friend, so every weekend, I traveled to Pittsburgh with one or two other teammates to be with him and his family as he gradually recovered and finally returned to college. He has always been an inspiration because he never gave up. Most men would have succumbed or become handicapped, but through hard work and God's grace, Bobby recovered, and a few years later he became a great pastor, husband and father, and to this very day, Bobby is my best friend."

Dove graduated summa cum laude with the class of 1963 and was accepted into Cornell University's joint Master of Fine Arts program in Creative Writing and the doctoral program in English Language and Literature. Just a few weeks ago he received his master's degree, but he has at least two or three years before he finishes earning his PhD. The really good news is that Dove won't have to be on campus most of the time. He has been writing articles and supplying photography for over a year for three magazines, which provided welcome income to support his assistantship at Cornell. He explained his writing and photo assignments were highly likely to continue for the next couple of years, and he may be traveling on assignment from time to time.

As Dove talked, Penny nodded her head silently listening to him describe his education and plans for the future. Penny realized studying at Cornell was a prestigious honor, and obtaining a doctorate there would be difficult. Yet, Penny knew Ithaca, NY was only three hours from Warren, and they would be together on weekends when he did not have to be on campus for classes.

Penny started to think about her desire to earn her master's degree too, and speculated she could complete her requirements while Dove was finishing his doctorate. St. Bonaventure University would be a terrific choice, as it was located between Ithaca and Warren. Penny told Dove of her plans to be the world's best teacher and pursue any courses that would help her achieve her objective. She had no desire to leave the classroom for administrative positions, as her desires were to teach grade school or biology, and set an example that will attract top quality people into the teaching profession.

Entering Warren, Dove questioned, "Penny, is that the sign you mentioned?" It proudly claimed Warren was home to 15,000 friendly people. Penny's arrival home was thrilling. Welcoming decorations were on the front porch, and several cars filled the long circular driveway when Penny and Dove arrived home from the Canadian Rockies. It was Wednesday afternoon, and Dr. Stevens met the new couple at the front door. Penny's brothers were there with their wives and children, and after kisses and hugs, Penny recognized a couple in the background she didn't know. Dr. and Mrs. Scott had driven to Warren from Grove City to meet their new daughter-in-law, and Dove hurried Penny over to complete the introductions. The gala was a fabulous homecoming for the new bride and groom, one that helped build friendships which lasted and grew stronger as the years passed. Before the afternoon was finished, Bobby and Christina Morris arrived to meet Penny, and Bobby agreed to be best man in the August wedding.

Chapter 16
Penny's Arrival in Warren

Penny told Dove the story about being deposited on the doorstep of Dr. Stevens when she was only five days old, and she sentimentally repeated stories of how the good doctor and his wife adopted and raised her as one of their own. "The Stevens had two tall and thin sons already in high school when I arrived, but I am the daughter they always wanted, but never had. Their large white two-story Federal style home had five bedrooms on the second floor. Mom and dad were happy to have a baby to energize their life, and from what I learned later — I filled the bill. Many times mom would say, 'Penny, you have made my life complete. I wanted a daughter more than anything, but one never came along until our lives were blessed when you arrived on our back porch.'"

"Come see what was left on the porch, Jake," Lois exclaimed as she removed the blanket and unwrapped the infant from her swaddling blanket. A talented nurse, she quickly examined the little girl while Jake was studying medical journals. She seemed to be splendid, her temperature was normal, and her skin was soft like Lois remembered Ron and Steve when they were infants. Her diapers were clean, and the pleasant smell of baby powder reminded her of her sons when they were babies.

Jake came around the corner and entered the kitchen. Seeing his wife with a precious bundle of joy, he said, "We best check her over good so let's bring her into the office." Jake adjusted his stethoscope and listened to the strong heartbeat, then checked the temperature and did a complete physical examination in less than five minutes. "Thank God, she's as healthy as any I've ever seen, and I've delivered hundreds of babies," Jake claimed.

Later that night Jake and Lois talked about the new baby and what they should do now. In those days doctors often found adoptive homes for abandoned infants, but they had been trying to have another child themselves for several years. Lois kept saying, "But Jake, this is an answer to my prayers, and I think we should report her to the county agents. I know they will allow us to keep her if we ask!"

On more than one occasion, Penny told Dove about growing up in this small town, in northwestern Pennsylvania, that she deeply loved. "The town isn't there any longer; oh the village is there, but it's no longer the same town." When Penny was small, Warren was a vibrant little community with a four story department store in the town center. People came to the county seat to work, do their business, and frequent a restaurant or shop.

Penny lamented, "Mom and dad keep talking about retirement, and they're thinking about moving to Florida. I'm going to miss them more than you can ever imagine." Her brothers were both doctors and practicing medicine in the Washington, DC area, and with Penny finished with college, there was little to prevent them from relocating.

After Penny related her origination story to Dove, he said, "Is this what they call a match made in heaven? I too was an orphan, but with less history than you." All Dove unquestionably knew was he was orphaned at an unusually young age, and he was given to a pastor with instructions to find a loving home. The pastor and his wife never relinquished him and instead adopted and raised Dove themselves. Perhaps working with orphans could be their calling, he thought as he cranked the cold engine on his Chevy Pickup truck.

Chapter 17
Penny's Memories of Warren

When Penny was a child, Warren was an incredibly beautiful little town of 15,000 friendly people, according to the large sign welcoming people to town. As youngsters, Penny and her friends joked about how many people there were in total if the unfriendly ones were included in the count. Located at the confluence of the Allegheny River and the Conewango Creek in northwestern Pennsylvania, this peaceful little town developed in the valley beneath the steeply sloped mountains on either side of the river. A statue of General Joseph Warren, a Revolutionary War hero from the Battle of Bunker Hill stood at the river's edge in downtown Warren, a persistent historical reminder of the town's roots.

The Allegheny Mountains surrounded the river valley and was important for the hardwood forests that were the main source of industry in the early 1800s. Massive white pine, hemlock and spruce trees, were harvested for flooring and structural components in the building trades. Mighty virgin forests of chestnut, maple, oak, hickory, beech and walnut trees were timbered and floated down the river to Pittsburgh and other cities. Fine furniture from Phoenix Furniture and Crescent Furniture Companies found its way to some of America's finest homes and filled the rooms inside many marvelous Victorian-style residences in Warren. These furniture factories were a dependable source of income for skilled woodworkers.

Oil was discovered in Warren in 1875, and a second explosion of growth ensued with the abundance of money for the owners of the wells. At one time, there were six oil refineries within six miles of Warren providing oil products to consumers in western New York and Pennsylvania. Good pay and secure jobs kept Warren expanding as other industries found their way to the village.

Wildlife was abundant, and the area became a fishing paradise by the time Penny was born in 1943. Hunters from Pittsburgh and neighboring Ohio towns filled the forest every fall seeking a trophy deer or cagey wild turkey, and trout fishing attracted sportsman in the spring and summer.

The town flooded too frequently as spring thaws melted the accumulated snows in the deep forests surrounding Warren. Penny could remember, as a girl, hospital evacuations using rowboats and small motor boats that saved people from the raging waters on the south side of Warren. She also recalled Beatty Jr. High School's athletic field and playground being submerged under ten feet of water.

Metzger-Wright department store, a four story building at the corner of Second Avenue and Liberty Streets, marketed nearly everything from notions, furniture and bicycles to clothing and cosmetics. Newell Press, a large commercial printer, provided advertising pieces for the famous New Process Company which was a giant mail order company in the downtown area that later changed its name to Blair. Retail stores closed on Wednesdays at 1PM and stayed open until 9PM on Friday only. Stores were all closed on Sundays, except pharmacies opened for a couple of hours after church. The second Thursday of every December, all ladies stores were opened to men only, and they offered free gift wrapping for Christmas presents.

Smith's Drug Store had an ice cream and soda fountain where a two scoop sundae with the works was only twenty-five cents. Flavored phosphates and cherry Cokes were the soft drinks of choice, made by some of the prettiest young girls in town. Two bakeries on the East side offered cream puffs and donuts along with fresh bread, which drew customers with the fragrance wafting from their ovens.

Finally after decades of planning and after moving the Cornplanter Indian reservation burial grounds in the early 1960s, the US Army Corps of Engineers erected a dam on the Allegheny River effectively making Warren and many cities along the river safe from flooding. The Allegheny Reservoir, a major recreation site, was created as water backed up from the dam into New York State. The dam was within five miles of Warren, creating a water recreation area that brought in fishers and boaters from around the Northeast.

Penny's face expressed pride and excitement as she told Dove about her home town she loved so dearly. Then, recognizing that she and Dove had never discussed where they were going to set up housekeeping, her expression changed. Dove noticed the different look in her eyes and a change in her voice, as tears came to her eyes.

Dove stopped her in mid sentence and queried her about her sudden change of demeanor. "Penny," he asked, "what's wrong? Have I said something that upset you?" He lifted her off the floor with his muscular arms, as he had that first night before he departed to sleep in the bed of his cold truck at Lake Louise. This time he kissed her full on the lips. Dove dried her eyes as she blurted, "Dove, can we live in Warren?"

Actually, until that very minute, Dove never considered where they would live. His position as a freelance writer was not location dependent, but he recognized after earning his PhD, Warren could be a problem. Still, that was in the future, and he had no real ties to Grove City. "We're going to live wherever you will be happy, and if it's Warren, then we shall be living in Warren. No more crying today Penny, we can live wherever you wish." That's when Penny said, "Love is good!"

Chapter 18
Penny's Childhood Memories

Penny told Dove of her first memories while she was with her mother at a downtown intersection in Jamestown, NY. "She had taken me about twenty miles from our home in Warren, PA to go shopping in a slightly larger city to the north. As they crossed the street, a large red city bus came down the steep hill and pulled up to the curb. A large black woman stepped from the bus. I was in awe! It was the very first black person I had ever seen and my eyes must have popped out of my head like kernels of popped corn exploding from the heat of the fire. I couldn't stop from gawking and following her movement as she stepped off the bus; and then the most incredible thing happened."

"The black woman stuck her tongue out at me, and she stared right back. The year was 1947, and I never forgot. She was a tall, hefty woman with a proud face and a determined look in her eyes. She wore a black hat and carried a giant long-handled handbag swinging from her arm. She did not plan passively to ignore my impolite gaze as she peered right back into my eyes.

Then, she vanished as fast as she appeared, but my memory of that encounter lasted a lifetime."

"I suppose I should have been forgiven for this dreadful act of intensely peering into this black lady's eyes and studying her pearl white teeth and smooth black skin, but the lesson was learned, immediately. No one had to tell me that it was reprehensible to stare at anyone who was different. My mother didn't have to tell me that it was inappropriate behavior; I knew it was wrong, even at four or five years of age. But she did tell me, and she explained there were people of many colors around the world and Jesus loves all the people."

"There were no televisions in Warren, and I had yet to visit a movie theatre. I didn't know there were people with different skin colors. The red and yellow, black and white we sang about at Sunday School didn't ring a bell yet. They were just words fit to music, and after all, I was only a little girl that didn't know better." As Dove listened to Penny's detailed account of her shopping trip with her mother, another reason occurred to him why he loved her. Penny took responsibility for her actions. No blaming others, just brutal facts and acknowledging she was wrong, remorseful, and she would never make the same mistake.

Penny lived in Warren until after she graduated from Warren Area High School in 1961, and began college at Penn State that fall. In those eighteen years, in Warren, she never knew of any black people living in Warren. Penny knew nothing about black people or Hispanics either, for that matter. Everyone was white in her little world the only differences were religion and ethnicity.

Penny explained to Dove, "I knew of families that were prejudiced against Catholics and Italians. As a matter of fact, thinking back, they were people who were less educated and often poor. I suppose they may have been trying to position their families above the social status they ever attained. I believe it is very difficult to understand how anyone concludes they are better than others, based solely on religion or when their family immigrated to the United States."

Penny continued, "I led a fairly sheltered life in Warren, but my first lesson on race was well learned in Jamestown. As a little girl, I determined if there is something about a person he or she has no control over, it is discrimination to consider those characteristics. People, for the most part, cannot change their skin color, eye color, height, physical handicap, weight or sex. Yes, they may be able to shed a few pounds, but I continue to believe many weight issues involve their DNA, and it is somewhat out of their control, or certainly difficult to control."

Fortunately for Dove and Penny, maintaining a healthy weight took little effort when compared with some of their friends. Dove agreed with Penny's analysis and he realized, for the most part, religious allegiances are determined by their families, and more people abandon religion than change to another faith. The more Dove thought about Penny, and recognized her deep morality, he realized, "I have married someone who understands life. She is a great catch!"

Chapter 19
The Swansons

Perle and Abel Swanson lived in a lower cost neighborhood on Warren's east side, near the United Refinery. They lived in a small, plain, white house with a large front porch and a small garden behind the home. They had five children, consisting of three boys and two girls, all living on the few dollars Perle made taking in laundry from several wealthy families in the downtown area, plus Fred's meager earnings as a school janitor at Beatty Junior High School.

By 1938, all of the Swanson children had dropped out of school, married and started their own families except for Maggie, their youngest and attractive daughter. Maggie had plans to be the first girl to graduate and only the third among her many cousins to complete twelve years of school. After school, Maggie helped with the ironing every day, therefore, she seldom had free time to join her classmates frolicking after school.

Her mother said Maggie had red hair, but Maggie claimed it was strawberry-blond. A case could be made for both points of view, because the summer's sun lightened Maggie's hair and at the same time made her angel kisses more pronounced than during the cold winter months. Her father took a particular shine to Maggie and claimed every freckle on her face was an Irish angel's kiss. Although Abel may have been sympathetic towards Maggie, he always supported Perle in family matters.

Maggie was tall and slender with large, Irish-green eyes and long dark brown eye lashes. Perle and Abel were intensely religious and kept to themselves except for church friends from their small evangelical Christian church. Although their four married children had left the church when teenagers, they were determined Maggie would grow up in the faith and make something of herself.

The little church they attended was often referred to as the "church of the don'ts!" "Don't do this and don't do that" seemed to be their utmost call. Many of these small evangelical churches were located in western Pennsylvania, but some were much more strict than others. Sunday was a day of rest, so noise or playing a sport was out of the question. Good Christians napped on Sunday afternoons, between attending two hours of the morning and another hour of evening worship services. Evening prayer services were conducted on Tuesdays and Wednesdays for another hour each. Dancing and jewelry were prohibited, and showing one's knees was an abomination for a woman. One local preacher claimed the color red should never be worn, and God had mandated he should never wear a necktie. Nearly all the members were older adults or young children, for most teenagers dropped out of the church as soon as possible.

Many female members of the little church wore their hair all rolled up in a tight bun and wore ankle length dresses. Musical instruments were not allowed in some churches, and that included a piano. Jewelry and make-up were often forbidden. Young ladies like Maggie felt restrained, and they exited the church as soon as they left their family homes and began their own families. Teenagers often rebelled and refused to attend church completely because of the strict rules, while others persuaded their parents to permit them to attend main-line protestant denominations rather than become totally unchurched. Fortunately, as the years passed, most of these small churches became less regimented and more lenient in their approach to Christianity, but some holdouts still clung to the nineteenth century rules.

Because of their rigid religious beliefs, the Swansons were not well liked by either neighbors or relatives, however, that didn't concern them whatsoever. They knew they were walking the "straight and narrow" road to glory, and the rest of the world was dammed to eternal hellfire and damnation. Although Maggie was friendly, attractive and smart, she too had difficulty maintaining close friends because of her parents' adherence to their religious beliefs.

Maggie was expressly forbidden to associate with Catholics and Italians, because her mother despised both groups of people. Although Abel was less bigoted than his wife, Perle was determined to keep a watchful eye on Maggie, and as she neared graduation, Penny began to rebel, just as her brothers and sisters did before.

Boys in her school didn't dislike Maggie, they just intuitively knew they did not want a life like Maggie's, so they gravitated to other more social girls. Because of her family, Maggie's home life was one of emptiness and misery. She loved the little town where she grew up, the schools she attended and her friends, but Maggie wanted to be more like her peers. Her mother used a different word to describe Maggie's desires:

"worldly." It was her mother and father who controlled her and forced her into denominational behaviors she did not believe.

Maggie sought escape from the confinement of her family, her church and Warren PA. She dreamed of a knight in shining armor who would take her to a life free from a controlling church and parents with their version of life's answers. This savior would release her from those who preached a life of "no" — no love, no joy, no hope and no faith in God's Grace. The Swansons just could not accept that God's Grace is free and not earned.

Chapter 20
Jon Davidson – Before the Gift

Jon Davidson drove north on US Route 62 that inclement spring day in 1943. His wife, Maggie, God Bless her soul, had died the night before of complications from childbirth and consumption, and he was in horrendous pain, having lost the only love in his young life. Jon's internal conflict was more than painful; he was fearful as he reconsidered his options about what would happen to his babies now. How could life be so unfair and so filled with sorrow? Why did he choose Maggie for his wife, and offer her nothing but heartache and grief?

Jon met Maggie three years earlier on a warm and sunny September day at the Warren County Fair in Youngsville, PA. He was waiting to purchase some cotton candy when he spied Maggie talking to some of her high school friends while standing on the banks of the Brokenstraw Creek. He was never sure what attracted him to her, but Maggie's radiant smile lit up his life in a heartbeat. "Yes," Jon thought, "it was the smile that enticed him to linger as her soft voice and attentiveness to her friends captured his imagination." Maggie was planning to graduate from Warren High School the following spring, and she already had a job lined up at the Warren National Bank beginning in June. She was the first person in her family to excel and graduate from high school. One could see the passion in her eyes as she explained the potential of a career in finance.

"I'm Jon Davidson," he interrupted, "and I'd like to buy a cotton candy for you." She was friendly, nevertheless rather hesitant at first, but one of her friends gave her a little push and said, "Maggie, go ahead, we'll see you later." As they ate their treat, Jon told her that he lived in Franklin and worked as a caretaker in a cemetery there. Maggie and Jon walked throughout the fairgrounds, stopping occasionally to greet another of her many friends. They viewed the freshly preserved jars of vegetables, fruit, and the livestock exhibits, while casually noting the blue ribbon winners. Maggie and Jon had a delightful Sunday afternoon that sunny day, and nervously, he proudly asked, "May I drive you home in my old but reliable 1933 Chevy Eagle with a rumble seat?" She was rather reluctant, but finally consented, but only on the condition he drop her off a few blocks from her house, so she could walk home alone. Obviously, she was afraid to take Jon home or allow her parents to know she had been in a car with him.

When they parted, Jon sensed Maggie would be his wife someday. From that day forward until today, the day she died, Jon never saw another girl who could turn his head. He was smitten! Maggie had to be sneaky to prevent her parents from finding out about Jon, but she liked him and devised a way to meet him every Sunday. Getting together was never easy because Jon worked long hours, and the drive to Warren was over an hour each way; nevertheless, they spent nearly every Sunday together and eventually married in December of 1940, five months after she became pregnant.

Jon's memories of their courtship were mixed with joy and shame and a sense of guilt about the outcome of their conduct. He felt he had caused her to lose all contact with her family. Jon knew her parents were evangelical Christians who had no tolerance for people not schooled in the straight and narrow path, but he wooed her and destroyed her life because of his own selfish physical needs. Jon was perplexed by the Swanson's code of ethics whereby it was customary to pray the Lord's Prayer each Sunday in church, and ask forgiveness for their sins, yet they were unable to forgive their daughter for her transgressions. He never had an opportunity to know the Swansons well, but he was sure Perle was so cold butter wouldn't melt in her mouth. Jon was not a particularly religious man. He seldom attended church, but he felt he could have been a much better person. He knew that and fully admitted his many shortcomings. Now he wished he would have been more sensitive to Maggie's needs, and less interested in violating her beliefs and tearing her away from her parents.

His Maggie was bed-bound while she suffered through the last stages of tuberculosis. Her chronic cough was dreadful as she gasped for every breath during the last few days of her short life. Sometimes she coughed blood, and often she had fearful night sweats with high fevers. The last month of her pregnancy Maggie lost weight as her delivery date approached.

Jon promised to care for their daughter, always love her and treat her with respect; but Jon and Maggie had sinned and there could never be forgiveness from the Swansons, particularly her mother, Perle. Jon guessed they were getting what they deserved for their iniquitous choices in life — but they would not receive the loving grace that God bestowed upon the Swansons for their sinful choices in life. In Jon's mind, grace was free.

Although Jon found it easy to avoid the Swansons, Maggie never recovered from the shame she felt for her unforgivable sin. In the Swanson home, forgiveness was weakness. Never yield to one who breaks the rule, and always persuade others to castigate offenders. Cast them out, so you will not be influenced by their behavior. Don't mingle with sinners or you will become like them. This was the law of the righteous Swansons! Maggie suffered the loss of her parents, her relatives, all of her friends, and all she received in return for her union with him was an underachiever who could have been more worthwhile.

Jon decided the two only decent things about himself were that he was faithful, and he truly loved Maggie. Still, he was a terrible husband. Jon wasn't the husband, provider, friend or lover he should have been. Jon and Maggie lived with Ruby, his mother, in a small upstairs apartment they shared. He could have provided more, but he loved working in the cemetery, caring for the grass, trimming the trees and shrubs and digging the holes to bury the dead. Looking back, he could have started a landscaping business and provided much more for Maggie, but he chose the easy way out. Now, Jon and his babies must suffer the terrible consequences of life without a wife and mother.

As Jon drove to Warren, he noticed the whitecaps had increased on the river as the winds strengthened and the snow began to drift along the roadside. Jon had an important duty to perform today, and then he could close the door on this part of his life — the life he had so miserably destroyed.

Chapter 21
Death of Maggie After Childbirth

As Maggie lay dying in the hospital room which overlooked the Allegheny River in Franklin, PA, she recalled living in Warren and the happy life she had there until she wounded her parents with her actions. Forgiveness was never easy for her family, and often family feuds lasted years before a truce was established. She thought about her demanding mother and the loathing episodes with her sisters, because of some unfulfilled expectation. Maggie's family struggled with control issues, and her mother was the most dictatorial of all. Her authority was rarely opposed because she would strike out in a fit of rage and quit speaking to the offender, sometimes for years.

This day, April 15, 1943, Penny was five days old. This was the day her mother, Maggie would die. Maggie was never permitted to see her daughter because of her disease, and the fear of infecting the infant with TB. Breathing was extremely difficult as Maggie remembered her family sending her away when they learned she was carrying Jon's child. Her parents never forgave, regardless of her many trips back to Warren, when Maggie begged, on hands and knees for forgiveness. There was no absolution in the Swanson family, and Maggie concluded she was cheated out of her childhood by her parents and the church doctrine they followed. Sporadically, she thought her parents were partially at fault for her great sin, because they made her life miserable and forced her to make choices she may not have otherwise made. Yet, she knew she made some terrible decisions in her life, and she took responsibility.

One year after her son, little Jon, was born, Maggie's parents, Perle and Abel Swanson died in a flaming auto accident, removing any hope of reconciliation or mercy, and Maggie was never able to remove the pain from her heart. Maggie forgave her parents, but her parents never absolved her of her great sin.

Still, Jon could not understand how the Swansons were unable to implement the Bible lesson of the woman caught in the act of adultery, when Jesus answered the stoners, "If any one of you is without sin, let him be the first to throw a stone at her." Certainly the arch-conservative evangelical Swansons knew better! Even Jon, admittedly a sinner, knew this commandment of Jesus.

His beloved Maggie certainly had nothing to live for on this earth, save her two children, but the God she trusted and loved was more understanding and forgiving than those on earth who judged her so harshly. As she struggled for every breath, she was comforted knowing her life would soon be over. Maggie died broken hearted, having lost every consequential thing in her life. First her parents, and then her best friends deserted her in her time of need. Now she was losing her newborn baby, Penny, to complete strangers. Penny was seized from Maggie before she could hold her close or even see her tiny face, and she struggled with the unfairness of life. When Maggie closed her eyes for the last time, her young son was gone from her side too. Only her husband remained by her bed, waiting for Maggie to succumb to her incurable illness. Tears flowed from Maggie's eyes as she thought about her happy days in Warren, when she was a popular young girl with friends and relatives who loved her. The God of Love would take away her tears, remove her pain, and comfort her in the hollow of His hand. This promise she truly believed.

Her husband, sat at her bedside listening to her labored breathing, her continuous gasps for air. Jon grieved for this troubled soul, raised in an unforgiving world. Maggie's only theological relief came from attending Religious Education Class one hour every Friday afternoon when she was in high school. Jon remembered her proudly recall, "Our small church did not participate in the R/E program, so I was assigned to the Presbyterian Church class. What a surprise to me as I viewed the marvelous gothic building and heard the teacher speak of the clear dichotomy between right and wrong. She made the argument that, in actual living, the decision is often a choice between bad and worse. I had been taught all these years that doing the right thing guaranteed happiness, but I knew better! Instead of living a perfect life, I came to accept the fact that God loves me when I'm good, and He still loves me when I have gone astray." Jon knew life was not always fair, and he deeply regretted the myriad ways he had contributed to Maggie's early demise.

During her death struggle, Maggie dreamed of Warren and her happiest moments there. Only her little babies had any hope of lives filled with happiness, and she would never be able to see their successes and pleasures. She dreamed of their circumstances, and saw beautiful images flutter through her mind of them living triumphant lives in the little town where the Conewango Creek joined the Allegheny River. She felt the hand of someone, perhaps the doctor or a preacher or maybe it was Jon, and she heard a faint voice pray, "May you have eternal peace and may God always be with you." Maggie had more faith than Jon, and now she was gone, and he felt remorse that he survived. As previously agreed, Jon would soon be taking Penny to Warren to seek a new home, and as Maggie closed her eyes for the last time, he released her hand, kissed her on the forehead and sobbed before he departed the hospital. No, Maggie's life wasn't fair, and she deserved better. Jon was troubled Maggie's life was better when she lived in Warren than when she lived with him, sharing a small apartment while she struggled with a fatal disease, and a beautiful small son. Though Maggie felt cheated from a happy childhood, her memories of Warren were better than the life he provided.

Chapter 22
Delivering the Gift

Warren was enduring a brutal cold spell on April 15, 1943. Winds were blowing from the west at thirty miles per hour, and heavy snow was beginning to drift as Jon Davidson headed north past Tidioute on Route 62. Snow trucks were out in force clearing the highways and spreading cinders to provide traction for motorists fearlessly heading to work. It had been another cold winter in northwestern Pennsylvania, with lake effect snow closing highways and schools several times during the winter. The good news was spring snows seldom last more than a day or two before thawing temperatures turned the white snow to dirty slush.

As Jon Davidson arrived in Warren that afternoon, he drove by Maggie's old house, but her parents had already passed away. Her other relatives had either moved away or died, leaving a void in his heart as Jon looked for a place to leave his priceless gift. It was Wednesday, and Jon needed to report to the Marine Corps on Monday, as he had been drafted. Jon had no wife, and no relatives, save his two babies and aging mother, and he needed to handle Maggie's last request. "Please, promise me that you will take Penny to Warren. I want her to grow up there with a loving family to care for her." Maggie took her last gasp and closed her eyes in eternal rest, leaving Jon with a beautiful little six and a half pound infant daughter just five days old and Jon, Jr., a hardy son just under two years old who could walk and talk every bit as ably as some four year old children. John remembered his mother's adage "he could walk and talk like nobody's business."

Jon couldn't help but feel shame. He had brought this trouble on Maggie by getting her pregnant, and he felt helpless watching her die. Her mother evicted her from their home as soon as they learned she was expecting a child out of wedlock. Jon did love Maggie, and he was devoted to her, but he was unable to provide for her as well as her parents. Now Maggie was gone, his mother was dying, and he was leaving for the Pacific theater to fight the Japanese. Oh, he could have probably gotten a reprieve from the draft, but Jon was desperate to leave the world behind and prayed someone would care for his precious babies. He just didn't see a way to solve his turbulent family issues other than joining the military, and hoping others would adopt his children, and care for them as their own.

Jon drove street after street in Warren, desperately searching for the right house with just the right people to place his precious gift, and then he suddenly knew the perfect location Maggie would have chosen. There was a small town just three miles from Warren where Maggie's family doctor lived. She always talked about what a wonderful man he was and how he was the finest doctor in the area. His office was in the parlor of a beautiful, white Federal style, two story residence overlooking the Conewango Creek. The office was closed that afternoon because Dr. Stevens always reserved Wednesday afternoons, to study medical and scientific journals. Obviously, the house was occupied as lights were glowing and he could see movement in the doctor's home.

Jon stopped the car and started to write a note to give to whomever adopted Penny. The least he could do was insure they knew her name and her date of birth. Jon stained the paper with tears streaming down his cheeks as he folded the brief letter and slipped it into a clean envelope.

There was a rear entrance into the residence with a large covered stoop and his mind whirled with completing the task. One last time, Jon changed Penny's diaper, and powdered her little body before giving his beautiful daughter one final heartfelt hug, and placing her back into her little homemade carrier. Then Jon tucked the note in the bottom of a cardboard box, and wrapped the blanket around the baby and set her inside the carrier. He folded the lid of the box to keep Penny warm and headed for the back porch of the beautiful white house.

Tears continued rolling down Jon's face as he rang the bell three urgent times, and then hurried to his waiting car. He paused to assure the doorbell was answered, and he saw a woman lift the box and carry it inside. Confident Penny was safely inside the home, Jon departed immediately, and headed back to see his son for the last time.

Chapter 23
Receiving the Gift

Jake Stevens loved to tell Penny about the day she came to live with Lois and him. He was such a gentle man who knew Penny loved to hear the story, over and over again. Dr. Stevens had finished his hospital rounds and completed the discharge papers for those well enough to return home. His office was closed Wednesdays, except for the occasional emergency, and frequently he even made a home visit to treat a patient who was unable to come to his office. This day, however, there was only one distraction from Jake's devoted reading time of catching up on the latest medical procedures and medications.

Only when he heard the piercing doorbell ring impatiently three quick times, did the doctor rise from his oversized desk chair, but he was already too late. His wife, Lois scurried to the back door, thinking an ill person needed prompt attention, but to her bewilderment no one was there. The entrance had a screen door that blocked her view of the small stoop's floor until she leaned forward, and peered down at the small cardboard box resting against the outside door.

She heard a car start, and saw it rapidly speed away once she answered the door, but the small box distracted her, and Lois could not recall the vehicle's make or even the color. Lois thought the car might be black, but it disappeared so quickly she wasn't positive. She forced the door open gently with her foot and retrieved the cardboard box.

Lois gently lifted the cardboard box and proceeded to the kitchen, not thinking a tiny baby was enclosed, however, she immediately recognized the sweet fragrance of baby powder. As she told the story, "You were there, Penny, wrapped in swaddling clothes and tucked inside a cardboard box, with your beautiful big blue eyes trying to focus on your new surroundings."

This day, as Penny sat in the chapel, she bowed her head and gave thanks for her parents. They could easily have called the police or handed the baby over to the county agents in charge of unwanted children. According to her mom, "There was absolutely no chance you would ever be sent away without a court order." Then Jake checked Penny over and said, "There's nothing wrong with this beautiful baby other than she has no parents to care for her."

As Penny lingered in the pew, that day, she dwelled on the words "care for" as her father was emphatic the note did not say, "I cannot love her," the note read, "I cannot care for her alone." Jake had already found the note in the bottom of the box. Over the years, he read that letter while he rocked his new baby daughter to sleep hundreds of times. Lois said tears welled in his eyes, and his voice cracked whenever he read the short painful letter aloud.

April 15, 1943

Dear Dr. And Mrs. Stevens:

I am unable to care for this beautiful child though I already love her very much. Her mother died early this morning, and I am leaving her in your trust. I pray God will direct your placement, so she has a happy life. We named her Penny. Her birth date was April 10, 1943. She weighed 6 pounds and 6 ounces. Please find a home for her, one that will provide love and joy to one so small and precious.

Thank you so very much for your consideration as you place my daughter. I do love her, I just cannot care for her alone.

Penny's Father

Penny loved to hear the letter read aloud because it clearly indicated her real parents loved her, but they were unable to care for one so small. Her birth mother was already dead, and her father was unable to raise her alone. Even as a small child Penny could understand that, thanks to her mom's caring explanation. On rare occasions, Penny wondered about her birth parents, but mainly, she wondered how they met, where they settled and where her birth father lived now.

Penny did not desire to meet him, but she would like to have known more about their lives, how they lived and died, and if there were other children from their union. Well, Penny realized she might never know about them, but once again she said a prayer for their lives and for hers too. There was never any question in her mind about having a better life with another family. Penny's parents treated her as one of their own children, and her older brothers treated her as a precious little sister.

Every time her parents introduced her they would say, "This is our beautiful daughter, Penny." She was immensely proud to be their daughter! She was also happy they called her their daughter, not their adopted daughter. Even today, as Penny dwelled on the subject, she believed it was cruel to call children: step-children, step-sister, half-brother or adopted child. Penny was her mother's little daughter, and the apple of her daddy's eye. She missed them, especially in her time of enormous loss, and Penny will always remember their undying love and affection for her.

Today was a day when remembering her parents allowed Penny an opportunity for relief. Dovie was always in her heart, but today she felt better prepared to accept whatever lies ahead.

Chapter 24
Jon Davidson – Leaving for War

Ruby Davidson was an old fifty-three years of age, already beginning to stoop when she stood. Her breathing was labored, and Jon wondered if she could have consumption too. He understood her reluctance to care for his babies, but he struggled with her inability to find a suitable foster home where they would be raised together. Jon returned to Franklin about suppertime in that oil permeated town on the Allegheny River. His son was awake from his nap, and playing in a corner with a red fire truck and Lincoln Logs his mother gave him last month for an early birthday present. Jon played with him, and tried to demonstrate how the fire truck's siren whaled, but the little boy was decidedly too young to comprehend, as he was too young to understand his mother had passed away, and his daddy would soon be gone.

Jon had a strange feeling as he boarded the train that he would never see his mother again, and tears flowed from his eyes as he thought of little Penny. Would he ever see his babies again, and if he did return from the war, would they want to see their father, the one who abandoned them?

Jon could not get his mind away from Maggie. Oh, how he loved her, even though he must have been a complete disappointment the nearly three years they were together. Maggie's thick reddish-blond hair still felt soft to the touch moments before they closed the casket lid, but now she lay in a cheap cold coffin beneath six feet of dirt. Certainly, it is difficult to think of himself as anything but a complete and dismal failure, and he couldn't help but wonder if Maggie's parents recognized a total loser when they saw him for the first time. Jon realized he should have done better for his family. He could have done better for his family. He can't forget or forgive his faults, and now it is too late to change. "Maggie would be alive today, if I hadn't ruined her life," Jon muttered under his breath as the conductor said, "all aboard."

The train whistled as it left the station, and Jon closed his eyes and cried. He had destroyed his beautiful Maggie, abandoned their two babies, and departed knowing his mother was near her deathbed. Jon feared he was a man whom even a mother could not be proud.

Chapter 25
The Death of Grandma Davidson

Ruby protested, "Not the door again, I can barely breathe when I sit here on the couch, and getting up becomes impossible anymore." The knock on the door was firm and loud on December 1, 1943. "I hope Jonny doesn't wake," she lamented, as she headed towards the door. "Are you Mrs. Ruby Davidson," a tall, well groomed sergeant asked. Two soldiers were standing at attention with a folded US Flag as Ruby opened the storm door. Immediately, when she saw the flag, she realized her son was dead, lost in an assault on some unknown remote Pacific Island. Sadness for herself struck first; then Ruby realized Jonny, her grandson, was an orphan with only a dying grandmother. World War ll was taking American men by the tens of thousands in Europe and the Pacific Theater, leaving parents and children alone in a treacherous world to cope for themselves. Her grandson would be alone now, without a single known living relative, for Ruby was unable to shed her tuberculosis and care for him.

Of course, there was the new baby girl that Jon picked up from the hospital when Maggie passed, but Ruby never knew where the baby was taken. Jon never brought her home because Ruby had the same disease as Maggie, and he would not risk Penny getting the sickness. She never saw Penny, yet her heart cried for her too. That's when Ruby first puzzled over how she could cope with Jonathan Davidson, Jr., or Dovie, as his beautiful, sweet mother loved to call him.

Ruby could barely care for herself as her breathing became more onerous, and with caring for a two year old orphan she could no longer cope. Ruby immediately called her pastor and told him of her son's death, his little son and her own acute illness. Pastor Scott and his wife Laura came to the house within thirty minutes and took charge of Ruby's situation. They called an ambulance to transport her to the hospital and assured her Jonny would be cared for until she was well enough to care for him again, but Ruby believed they knew she was never going to leave the hospital alive.

Ruby cried for her son and his two children, and she lost all hope for her grandchildren to live happy lives. She loved her son, and knew he was much too qualified for grave digging, but she was never able to convince him of the importance of increasing his earning power. Jon wanted to be a carefree outdoorsman and pursue a livelihood he loved. A week later Ruby was buried next to her husband in the exact cemetery in which Jon had labored before joining the Marines. Only two neighbors and the pastor's family were in attendance when her body was lowered into the dark grave.

Chapter 26
The Scotts

Dove never knew much of his birth mother or father. He had long forgotten any memories of their faces, and his grandmother passed away before his third birthday. The small boy was given directly to the Scotts as a foster-child, until the court was satisfied no one would protest their adoption. It was particularly common for ministers, lawyers and doctors to have significant influence on adoption proceedings; therefore, the skids were greased for a summary court remedy. A county judge approved Jon's adoption by the Scotts when he was three years old, then they left Franklin to minister to a larger church in Butler, PA.

Before leaving Franklin, the Scotts strategized about the best way to handle the adoption after they relocated, and they decided they would always refer to their son as Dove. No mention would ever be made that Dove was adopted, so friends and neighbors always assumed their son was their child from birth. There were no positive reasons they could conjure up that suggested using the word "adopted" made sense to them.

Certainly it was better for their son to be like other boys, and not be subjected to the torment of youth. They knew his grandmother called him Dove or Dovie; therefore, the Scotts used that name exclusively.

As the years passed, the Scotts transferred to new pastorates with an ever increasing circle of friends, and they had all but forgotten what little they knew of Dove's grandmother. They never met his deceased parents or the infant born just before Maggie died. Dove was theirs. They were dedicated to provide a loving home and a top-flight education.

The Scotts were a loving couple who had wanted a child from the beginning of their married life, but sadly God had never granted an answer to their years of fervent prayers. In 1943, Ron and Laura were both thirty-one years old, married for some nine years without conceiving a baby, and they were becoming desperate. Their friends, family and associates, were constantly asking when they would begin their family, and Laura fought depression after these frequent reminders of her or Ron's apparent infertility.

Laura had dreamed of a daughter since the days she played with her favorite doll, Annie, and wheeled her doll carriage up and down the sidewalk nearly every day. Laura was eager to teach her daughter how to bake and envisioned shopping trips for colorful, frilly dresses. Ron, on the other hand, was hoping for a son to carry on the family name and keep him company while fishing and hunting in the beautiful forests of western Pennsylvania.

When Dove came to live with them, Laura continued to pine for a daughter because the little boy did not fulfill her need to mother her own child. Dove gravitated towards his father because Ron was forever spending his time proudly displaying his new son to anyone that would listen.

After Dove's fourth birthday, Laura had an incredible surprise. Her years of prayers were answered and she realized she was pregnant, changing her life from one of despair to one of unimaginable joy. As soon as Laura learned she was to give birth to her own child, she became a different mother to Dove. Her new loving personality rubbed off on everyone, including her small son who willingly absorbed the new found love and attention from his mother.

Jenny was born on New Year's Day, 1946, the first baby delivered in the Butler General Hospital that year, and Dove had a new baby sister to share with his parents.

Chapter 27
The Stevens

The Stevens were incredibly happy when Penny's adoption was granted, not that they had doubts of final approval. Unlike the Scotts, Jake and Lois were already parents to two boys, thirteen and fifteen years old. At once, they realized there was no way to protect their new daughter from knowing she was adopted, for they lived a public life with family, patients, friends and associates. The word chosen became important, for they chose Penny to be their daughter, and they were thrilled over the rightness of their decision. There was never any doubt about the desire to make Penny their very own.

By the time Penny learned she was not born naturally to the Stevens, she realized she was loved every bit as much as her two older brothers, Ron and Steve. She was always introduced as their daughter or the boy's sister, never adopted daughter. The boys were too old to be regular playmates for Penny, but many times they stayed home to babysit when she was small.

Lois always wanted a little girl, and soon she decided she wanted to be a full-time mother again, and gave up her nursing duties. She was determined for her new daughter to excel academically, therefore, throughout Penny's grade school experience Lois was active as room mother and class baker. Wherever Lois went, Penny was soon to follow, and their closeness endured through school and Penny's college years.

When Penny was in high school, Dr. Stevens employed her in his home office on Saturdays. There was a large waiting room, and many patients had appointments; however, some people would just drop in unannounced, as the honorable doctor turned no one away. Often, when someone appeared to be quite ill, Penny would move them to the head of the line saying, "Mrs. Smith, the doctor will see you next. Room two please." Penny became as compassionate as her father; she always admired his patience and determination to diagnose the illness and provide a remedy. Often he dispensed medicine in the office, especially for those who were needy, and she would see him write no charge on their paperwork. She was sure his kindness, along with his medical knowledge, were the reasons his office was always overflowing.

Dr. Stevens continued to make house calls, and he delivered many babies at home, until he reduced his hours, and recruited a new doctor to Warren to share his practice.

Chapter 28
Preparing for the Wedding

A period of seven weeks is not long to plan and prepare a wedding. Because it was summer vacation at Grove City College, August 7 was an open date at the chapel. Reservations needed to be booked close to a year ahead, particularly in May and June when the new graduates often married. Thankfully, Lois Stevens and Laura Scott, Penny's mother and mother-in-law, worked tirelessly making the arrangements, while Dove and Penny stayed in the Canadian Rockies for an extra week.

The invitations were mailed on July 10, thanks to Penny's mom. She was so thrilled about the upcoming nuptials she personally picked out the cards, addressed and sent them to the 750 friends, and relatives of both families, along with the Grove City College faculty and staff. She was experienced with invitations as she did this nearly forty years before for her own wedding. Additionally, she helped both of her sons and daughter-in-laws plan their weddings, and she managed the responses.

Dove's mother, Laura lived in Grove City, so she made all of the decisions concerning flower arrangements for both the wedding and the dinner reception, and she hired a wedding coordinator. She worked countless hours with the planner as they organized the extensive and elaborate dinner following the wedding. The plan was for a large, but unpretentious wedding with only a few close friends or participants having specific roles.

Penny's father, Jake, got involved by contacting Dr. Martin Johns, one of his medical doctor friends, who lived in Grove City with his wife, Alice, to assist him in booking the reception dinner venue. Only a few years before, Jake and Lois attended an elegant wedding reception dinner for their daughter, and they wanted to use the same location. Alice was thrilled to be involved, and she arranged dinner for the four hundred people whose RSVPs were received. Dove attempted to impress Penny when he asked, "Do you know what RSVP means?" She pretended she had no clue and allowed Dove show off his knowledge of French. Dove's second language was French, and he was fluent as that was a requirement for his advanced degrees. "RSVP means: répondez s'il vous plaît, or in English, we say, please reply." She quipped, "You think you're pretty smart don't you." Penny pretended she never heard the definition, but she studied French in High School, and although she wasn't fluent in French, she did know the meaning of RSVP. For goodness sakes, Penny had been invited to parties many times that required a response. Before they were finished with the conversation, Dove knew Penny had been sandbagging him. He realized she was an educated woman and didn't climb out from behind a rock yesterday.

Penny and Jon were content to accept the decisions others made, because they were more interested in the wedding itself and the content, not the components involved in making a wedding occur. Dove and Penny also had the task of selecting their wedding attire. There was no second guessing or attempting to please everyone. She selected a full-length wedding dress with a tiny halter strap in matte satin with a top-stitched princess-line godet skirt with a long sweeping train. This elegant dress caught her eye immediately, and sight unseen, Dove blessed her decision. Dove rented his black tuxedo, with all the accessories, from the same shop, and they were finished in an afternoon. Only the final fittings remained to be completed.

Lois and Laura selected floor-length apricot dresses and oversaw the fittings for each attendant. Penny tried to express her appreciation for their willingness to free her from these duties, as she was about to begin her first day of teaching on September 7, and she was already working on lesson plans for her third grade students.

Penny's nephew, four year old Craig Stevens, would be the ring bearer and one of Dove's family friends volunteered their sweet little four year old as flower girl. The two children were a charming addition to the wedding. Craig dressed in a white tux contrasting against his tanned skin and dark brown hair, and Ginger with her long, flowing, blond hair in an apricot dress, matched the other female attendants' gowns.

Dove's and Penny's goals and expectations for the marriage were happiness and love, not the bickering atmosphere they had heard others endure. Perhaps it was just luck, or maybe it was predestination, but the Scotts and the Stevens genuinely liked one another, and they quickly made a terrific team. They only noticed cooperation and none of the controlling that so often creates tension and hard feelings. Everyone understood that the wedding was for the new Mr. and Mrs. Jon Scott, and they should have the final authority to change anything. There was no need for change, as the families worked together to provide the best support possible. And that support lasted until her last parent, and Penny's last brother passed away. She still misses them, even after all these years

Chapter 29
The Wedding

The morning sun shone brilliantly on the spire atop Harbison Chapel on Saturday morning, casting a long shadow over Rainbow Bridge spanning Wolf Creek as it meandered through the beautiful campus. The landscaping was manicured, and each building had a uniform gothic architectural appeal. The sanctuary was shaded as the sun was still low in the sky when Dr. Scott arrived at 7:30AM on August 7, 1965, to make final preparations for the wedding. He knew he had ample time before even the first person arrived, but he wanted to calm his nerves, and what better way to begin than with an early prayer.

Reverend Dr. Scott knew this wedding would be unusual, for both Dove and Penny were connoisseurs of classical music. As children, both played multiple instruments with precision, a routine both continued until they finished college. Ron, as the Dean of the Chapel, knew many of the greatest wedding scores ever written were penned by history's most accomplished composers. He also knew the most talented musicians to perform those scores.

Penny and Dove were just stirring when Ron left the parsonage, so he didn't have an update concerning any final details needing his attention. Weddings were common at the chapel, and he officiated in most and participated in all, as he was the Chaplain at Grove City College, a most prestigious calling. Dr. Ron Scott was always prepared and never nervous when he offered sermons, memorial eulogies or wedding vows, but today was different.

The Stevens and the Scotts were prominent families, and the invitation list was long, and included many local notables. Folks from surrounding towns where Ron had pastored for the past thirty years, plus college professors and staff from Grove City College would assuredly be in attendance. Of course, the bride and groom had many close friends planning to attend the wedding. Yes, this was an important social gathering, perhaps the most important of the year, save graduation ceremonies in May.

The chapel was alive with activity by 10AM as cleaning people, florists, musicians and the marriage director all hustled to make everything picture perfect before the bride was escorted down the aisle on the arm of her father. Ron was proud and excited that he was asked to perform the ceremony, but now that the day had arrived, he rather wished he were a special guest like his wife, Laura, watching the celebration from the front pew.

The ceremony was to be a basic Christian wedding in which the bride and groom pledged their love and fidelity to one another, followed by Holy Communion as their first joint act of devotion to God. This was the part that concerned him. He knew Penny and Dove had been living together for the past seven weeks and were already legally married. Many, if not most of the attendees, knew of their Canadian marriage and relationship, and Ron wanted to be careful presenting the couple appropriately.

He had qualms proclaiming them as the "new" Mr. and Mrs. Jon Scott, but he still had some time to decide the announcement's wording. Remarkably, Ron and Laura knew little of their new daughter-in-law; however, they had seen glimpses of why Dove had so quickly given his heart to this beautiful woman with the long, coal-black hair and blue eyes that sparkled like stars in the heavens. Already she had impressed Laura with her wit and her desire to help children, particularly orphaned or abandoned children. Laura knew there was an urgent need to help those less fortunate who were unable to care for themselves.

The organist was practicing Bach's beautiful *Air on a G String* while the florist was bringing floral arrangements into the chapel. The vocalist was in a small rehearsal room, in the basement, warming up by intoning the notes of the music scales. Many guests started to arrive shortly after noon, occupying their time by photographing the campus, especially the Crawford Hall administration building, Buhn Library and of course Harbison Chapel. These three exceptionally attractive gothic buildings drew the crowd's focus as they surveyed the picturesque campus in the small town of 8,500 people.

Time seemed to evaporate as Ron heard the chapel music begin in preparation for the guests. The organist's instructions were to commence playing the old four manual Kimball organ thirty minutes prior to the service. Classical wedding music echoed throughout the chapel as guests arrived and were escorted to an appropriate pew. At exactly 2PM, Dr. Andrew Jefferson, Professor of Organ and Piano began the ceremonial music with *Jesu, Joy of Man's Desiring*, sung by soprano, Dr. Ann Toil. Jared Parish, an incredible senior tenor, sang *If*, made popular by the group "Bread." The third solo was *The First Time Ever I Saw Your Face*, sung by Robert Pasco, a brilliant new voice instructor at the college. The selection was a reminder of the first words Dove spoke to Penny when he said, "I'm so sorry I didn't mean to stare, but I have never seen such a beautiful face in my entire life!"

Other arrangements included Pachelbel: *Canon In D for Trumpet Voluntary*, and, of course Wagner's *Wedding March* which accompanied the beautiful bride as she processed down the aisle on the arm of her proud father.

Dr. Scott lifted the wedding rings from the small apricot colored satin pillow being held by Penny's nephew, Craig, and held them high for all the attendees to view. Dr. Scott then delivered a brief history of the wedding ring stating, "For thousands of years, lovers have exchanged rings as a token of their love. First, they were made of reeds that grew along the fertile Nile, then of bones, later of iron and finally gold. These gold bands are made valuable by the unity represented in the wearing of them, not because of the gold they contain. Because of an ancient Greek conviction, the rings are worn on the third finger, because a particular vein led from the finger directly to the heart. The ring is the symbol of unity in which your lives are joined in one unbroken circle. Always remember that a ring, like a circle, has no beginning and no end, no giver and no receiver. Wherever you go, you will return to one another. May these rings remind you of the promises you make to one another today. The rings you now present to each other are the symbols of the endless love you offer each other as husband and wife." At that point, the bride and groom placed their gifts of gold rings on each other's fingers.

Penny then looked Dove directly in the eyes and pledged: "On this splendid summer day, I pledge my love to you, Dove. You have given me joy since the moment we met. You have given me hope, and you have given me love. Poetry is not my forte, but I feel something inside that is more powerful than words. This something has wrapped itself around my heart and won't let go, it bonds to my very being and holds me close whether you are near or far. Dove, my pledge to you is of eternal love, like the ring on my finger it has no beginning and no end. My life is your life, and wherever you go, you will always have me near, for I will cling to you as a mother to her child, and I will always be there when you beckon. I fervently love everything about you and everything you do."

Dove then looked at Penny when he pledged, "Penny, you are now even more beautiful than when I first beheld you on that magnificent mountain top in the Canadian Rockies. Every day with you is like viewing the world with new eyes, seeing more clearly, and feeling more deeply and loving more dearly. I promise you today, Penny, that I will always love you, always respect you, and always try my very best to make you happy we fell in love and committed our lives to one another for as long as we both shall live." There was a slight pause which sounded like he wanted to add one more thought that had just entered his mind. He continued, "I have never been as happy as I am at this very moment, and it is all because of you and who you are."

Holy Communion is seldom seen in weddings at the chapel, however, following the exchange of vows, the young couple followed Reverend Dr. Ron Scott to the steps leading to the altar table and in view of the entire congregation they received their first communion together, their first act of marriage. When Penny and Dove rose after Communion, Dr. Scott introduced the couple as "my son and daughter-in-law, Mr. and Mrs. Jon Scott, of whom I am incredibly proud." The music, Handel's *La Rejouissance* was used for the recessional, and the attendees awed at the outstanding performances by every musician. The wedding was a success in every way, one many attendees would remember for a lifetime, as it was highlighted by such heavenly music.

Beginning at 6PM, all invitees attended a lovely formal dinner at the magnificent Grove City Hotel followed by dancing to the music of a five piece orchestra until the wee hours of the morning. Dr. Stevens toasted Penny and Dove, "To Mr. and Mrs. Jon Scott, known to everyone here as Dove and Penny. May they live a life filled with the love they feel tonight, and may their love spread throughout people in our land and even to the ends of the earth. As Dr. Scott toasted earlier, our families and friends are incredibly proud of Dove and Penny. May love glow in their hearts throughout their entire lives as it radiates tonight."

Certainly it was a stressful day, but it could not have been better. Soon, after she danced with her father, Penny and Dove withdrew from the reception, and headed for Pittsburgh to catch a morning flight to Hawaii, where they continued their dream of love for six days of fun in the sun. Dove kept saying, "Love is good! Penny, Love is really good."

Chapter 30
Penny's Greatest Loss

This morning Penny could hear Charles Wesley's hymn, *And Can It Be That I Should Gain,* as a student prepared on the organ for the upcoming chapel program. That beautiful old hymn resonated within as Penny thought of the wondrous words and promise of the lyrics. She had heard the hymn here before and recalled the students singing this difficult musical piece in perfect harmony. Their performance revealed the hymn was among their very favorites as tears glistened in many student's eyes. Dove and Penny had discussed the compulsory short principled chapel programs held each week on Tuesdays and Thursdays where Christian music preceded a short message of fifteen or twenty minutes. Additionally, a Vespers service was held every Sunday evening during the school year. Penny often attended the service since retiring from teaching because the chapel meetings were so uplifting and the speakers inspiring.

It was a dreary day with dark storm clouds overhead, and pounding rain streaming off the roof and splashing to earth.

Fog and light rain cycled onto the campus area until the skies finally blackened, while thunder rumbled and lightning streaked the afternoon sky, frightening scores of prayerful visitors. Today Penny's saddest memories tortured her mind, perhaps due to the dreary and violent weather. Her lost baby was her focus as she dwelled on her miscarriage.

Her thoughts brought visions of Dove and her quietly celebrating their third wedding anniversary, when she first realized she might be pregnant. Penny wouldn't claim they were trying to have a baby, but they weren't using any precautions to prevent the beginning of a new life either. Thinking about it in the chapel this morning, she guessed they both knew they were hoping for a child, but were reluctant to admit their hopes, even to one another.

Penny and Dove debated the date they should commemorate their anniversary because of the two weddings, and decided they would celebrate both weddings, June 21, and August 7. Both dates had special meanings for them for different reasons. June 21 was the beginning of a commitment to one another, ending only when her Dovie passed away. August 7 was the day they announced their commitment for all to hear in a formal setting. Privately they celebrated on June 21, and with others on August 7.

They were at a small, out of the way, quaint little restaurant called Pinewoods enjoying their exceptional Friday night special of fried haddock with cold slaw and French fries. They tried to avoid fried food, but this place was unusual and known countywide as the greatest fish fry in the area. It was there Penny first mentioned to Dove that she might be pregnant. Penny wasn't totally sure, but she was three weeks late and generally, Penny was as regular as the full moon. They were both excited and began to discuss how their lives would take on new dimensions and directions if they were blessed with a baby.

Dove was well on his way to completing his doctorate at Cornell University, so the timing was fabulous. He had completed all of his required class work and was ready to defend his thesis. He was confident he could finalize everything within a few months, and be known as Dr. Jon Scott.

They spent hours considering their future child's name and hunting for the crib, dresser and clothes he or she would need. Dove never admitted it, but he wanted a little boy for his hiking and fishing buddy. Penny knew that any boy would bear the nickname of Buddy. She, on the other hand, was secretly hoping for a baby girl to dress in frilly clothes, flowers, and buttons and bows. Penny's choice of name was Missy, short for Michelle!

After dinner, they went to Penny's parent's home for dessert as they did every June 21, reliving the joy they found together on that mountaintop in 1965. Telling them she was pregnant later that night was one of the most exciting times of her young life. They were so thrilled they were calling her brothers and some of their friends before Penny and Dove left for home; and Jake called Dr. Thomas at his home to make an appointment for Penny to have a complete physical on Monday after school. Of course, they called Dove's parents and his sister, Jennifer, and conveyed the exciting news; and it was obvious they were overjoyed to have their first grandchild on the way. Having such wonderful and supporting parents still makes her proud today, more than forty years later.

Until the fourth month, Penny didn't appear pregnant, but in time her clothes started to be snug around her waist, and it was noticeable to the discerning eye that she was with child. Those days were some of the happiest of Penny's life, planning for a new generation of the Scotts. They were so excited to have an opportunity to raise a child with the love and guidance they had been so fortunate to receive as children. Then distressing news suddenly took Penny's joy and filled her heart with despair.

Penny had no discomfort until her fifth month, when she awoke at 2:10AM on November 4 with a stabbing pain in her lower abdomen. The ambulance arrived within minutes, but before Penny reached Warren General Hospital the pain subsided. Unfortunately, Penny lost the baby and was never again able to become pregnant. Dove and Penny both suffered terrible sadness and felt depressed about life for several months until they accepted their fate was to be childless. Dove took to writing many hours in his study, and Penny's teaching responsibilities required significant preparation time. Their time consuming occupations briefly helped them replace their regrets with the distraction of work.

Penny fought the depression that accompanies this type of incident, and with her family, particularly her mother, she was able to put her grief aside and continue with life. Still, Penny refused to believe she could never have her own child, and she fought that fear and emptiness for many years, suffering acute mental distress. Dove suffered as well, and yet he cared for Penny like someone trained for easing the pain of the loss of a child. Penny grieved, but she also rejoiced in having Dovie and her parents with her, to help overcome her anguish and distress.

Penny had few other disappointments in her life, but losing their baby and never being able to give Dovie the children he so richly deserved was a crushing sadness from which she never fully recovered. Still, she knew most marriages have profound issues that make theirs seem tepid. They struggled through the pain and concentrated their efforts to help other people's children get through the pain of rejection, when they were outcast from their families.

That day, the storm clouds cleared before Penny departed the chapel, much like her sadness dissipated. Time spent alone in the chapel was a healing time for Penny, and she continued to visit the chapel every week. She always felt relief when she walked out the massive front entrance and headed home.

Chapter 31
The Stone Quarry

Saturdays were days when Dove and Penny selected some area to hike for a few hours before duties like laundry, cleaning and mowing were considered. Sometimes they drove to Sheffield to an area referred to as the "Virgin Timbers." The area was reachable only after dry spells, even with their four wheel drive truck. Most area forests were harvested over one hundred years before, but there was one unharvested area they loved to explore. Large areas of hardwood trees like oak, maple, cherry and beech provided food for wild turkey, squirrel and black bear. Only the "Twin Sisters" gas lines and maintenance service roads intruded into the wilderness. They always carried compasses and stayed together to prevent losing their way in this gargantuan timber area. Other forests surrounding Warren contained mature trees, but nothing compared to the area near Sheffield where trees measured more than six feet in diameter.

Dove and Penny went to her parents to enjoy Thanksgiving with her family in 1970, five years into their marriage. They lived outside Warren in a small, but beautiful Cape Cod home on twenty acres, mostly composed of mature hardwoods, which they harvested, for their fireplace firewood. They spent one holiday with Penny's parents, and one with Dove's parents because the Scotts ministry required them to be in their church for holiday services. As much as they tried, God had not seen fit to grant them a child, but they continued to enjoy each other's company along with hiking new areas.

Penny had completed five years of teaching at the Market Street School, and Dove continued to do freelance writing and photography, but he was nearing completion of his first novel, a story about Appalachia and the difficulty leaving for more upscale environs. He had earned his PhD two years earlier and was constantly recruited to teach college. After Thanksgiving dinner, Dove and Penny decided to take a hike in an area they had never explored. Penny's brothers were in Warren for the holiday with their families, but they wanted to spend more time with his parent's, so Dove and Penny took their kids and headed toward the east side of Warren and parked near the intersection of Branch Street and Jackson Avenue. The climb was modest as they picked up an old logging trail that paralleled Jackson Avenue for a couple of hundred yards, and led to a walking trail that headed towards higher ground. They knew Jackson Avenue met Fifth Avenue about three miles to the east, so they were surrounded by roads. Certainly they couldn't get lost. They had been out of the car for less than thirty minutes when they came across an old stone quarry that faced south. The United Refinery and Sylvania Electric were two critical manufacturing plants in clear view. They were located down in the valley, in an area often referred to as Glade. The Allegheny River was gently flowing in the background. They decided to scale the outcropping of large rocks and loose stones when Dove noticed some engraving about one-quarter of the way up on the left side of the quarry.

His voice became excited when he said, "Penny, hurry over here and see this engraving." There on the face of the giant, gray rock surface, it appeared someone etched "Otto Dove" in elegant script. Demonstrably, Otto Dove had chiseled his name in the stone, perhaps a century before. Initials like JD, WD, HD and FD were also carved in much smaller block type versions. Not being an expert in engraving stones, their guess was the weather had smoothed the corners over the decades until the script looked like fancy penmanship.

"Didn't you tell me there were some Doves in Warren," Dove asked. Then Penny remembered that it was the day they met, when they introduced themselves to one another. She felt that warm feeling in the pit of her stomach as she thought about that marvelous day high in the Canadian Rockies, when Dove nearly panicked and ran away after telling Penny that she had the most beautiful face he had ever seen. What young lady could ever forget that? Then, she dwelled on the fabulous good fortune they had that day when they stumbled into an everlasting love in a place neither of them would ever forget.

Later that day they opened the phone book and observed there were some Doves still residing in Warren, but none of Penny's family knew any of them. When they went to bed that night, Dove said, "You know Penny, I had a marvelous day today. Seeing your brothers and hiking with their children was great. Sometime I'm going to learn more about how they were able to move those stones from the quarry down off the side hill, and how Otto Dove was able to produce such a beautiful engraving in the stone. Maybe there's a novel in there someplace."

"Well, doctor," Penny quipped, "I had a wonderful day too. Next week, let's rent a canoe, and put in at the Kinzua Dam. If the weather holds, we can paddle down to Warren or even Irvine, and I'll tell you about the time I became lost in a remote area up the Kinzua Creek, when I was separated from my hiking friends. This is hard to believe, but I was only fourteen years old, and I walked all the way to Ludlow through some major forests. I dreaded the thought I would have to spend the night alone in the deep woods. Just before darkness overtook the fading light, I saw some headlights coming around the side of a hill ahead. You can bet your life that mom and dad were furious with me for going off on my own! Maybe there's a novel in there too!"

Chapter 32
Jill Harrison

Jill was everyone's friend, one of the prettiest and brightest high school kids Penny ever knew. Jill was in Penny's first period biology class when she was a sophomore during the 1971-72 school year, and Penny was in her second year teaching at Warren Area High School after completing five years working with third graders. Jill was a student that participated in class, and she always had something worthwhile and well thought out when she engaged.

Her family were dairy farmers that were up at the crack of dawn or sooner to milk the small herd, before she cleaned up and boarded the school bus. Her father had a day job at Sylvania Electric where he worked in the maintenance area doing electrical and production set-ups, as required. Her mother worked part-time at Betty Lee, a small woman's retail apparel shop in Warren, which enabled her to ride to work with her husband on her workdays. Among their jobs and the farm, they earned a modest income and always lived within their means.

After Christmas break ended, Jill met a new student that swept her off her feet resulting in her schoolwork being neglected, causing lower grades and little interest in school. By early March, Penny met privately with Jill to question her about her change of attitude towards school and her plummeting grades. While they discussed her grade in biology they also talked about her other classes too, and within a few minutes Jill broke down and started to wail uncontrollably.

Penny patiently waited for Jill to calm down, and then Penny attempted to console her, as she explained it was not too late to improve her grades. It was then that Penny learned Jill was pregnant and had not confided her condition to anyone, even Jason, her new boyfriend. She had been under duress, not daring to tell anyone and suffering from severe anxiety for weeks. This was a situation where Penny was totally out of her comfort level, and she was not sure how to respond to Jill's need. She said, "Jill, I'm not sure how to advise you at this moment, and I truly need some time to think this through." They talked another half hour before agreeing to meet the next afternoon. Penny promised that their conversation was confidential and that she would try her best to help Jill through this overwhelming trial.

Jill was terrified to inform her parents, because although she was convinced she loved Jason, she was not ready to marry anyone. She explained her father had high expectations for her, and he would be distraught beyond imagination. Her mother seldom made family decisions, and Jill was sure she would follow her husband's lead. Jill simply didn't know which way to turn, or to whom.

Thank goodness Dovie was home that night, and so were her mom and dad. Penny needed help in order to provide the alternatives Jill required, and she needed help soon. Penny's parents came over that night, and without revealing names, she asked everyone to consider the possible alternatives she could convey to Jill, and how they might be able to assist her.

All four had talked for nearly an hour before Penny started to take notes. They each raised possible solutions, and Penny noted the pros and cons for each; and when they were finished they had ten recommendations which might help Jill through her trial. They considered everything from having Jill tell her mother first in order to solicit her help with her father, to getting the school nurse involved. Penny asked her dad if he would assist, because she knew her father was their family doctor. Jill mentioned that her father had been to Dr. Steven's office on several occasions, as recently as three months ago regarding a leg he had injured two years earlier.

The more they talked, the more they realized there were no easy solutions, but they agreed on five scenarios, and Penny prepared for the meeting, after school. The preferred solution was the solution Jill like best too, and that was to get the school nurse to be present when Jill informed her parents of her pregnancy. Jill wanted Dr. Stevens there with the nurse when she made the revelation, hoping to keep her father calm.

The next day, Jill's parents were asked to come to school for a meeting in the nurses office. Later, her father told Penny it was a difficult meeting as Jill confessed her actions to her mother and father. Jill begged forgiveness and was immediately embraced by both parents as tears flowed freely from their eyes. The school administration agreed Jill could finish her sophomore year, and the family would determine an appropriate way for Jill to give birth to her new baby.

Jill struggled with guilt for many months after revealing her pregnancy to her mom and dad, and Penny met with Jill after school each Friday. They talked about taking responsibility for the woman she would become. There was nothing she could do that would make her feel better about what she had done before the baby was born, but after the baby arrived, Jill would take control over her life once again.

Jill was forgiven by her parents and other relatives, but she wrestled with forgiving herself for the actions which would change her life. She was quick to take responsibility for what she did, but she was unwilling to forgive herself and move on to the next stage of her life. She also admitted she was not prepared to be a mother and care for an infant. With her parents' guidance and Penny's encouragement, Jill decided to permit her baby to be adopted. The baby was removed from her immediately after birth to prevent her from becoming attached to the little boy, who was promptly adopted.

Penny believed time was a great healer. Poor Jill grappled over her poor judgment for five years before she completely forgave herself and moved on with her life. As time passed, Jill pursued a career with the New Process Company in Warren. She refused to date again until after a female friend was killed in a gruesome multiple car accident on a dangerous overpass near Irvine. Jill helped with her two little preschool boys while their father worked second shift at The National Forge, a major employer in the area. Eventually, Jill married her friend's husband and adopted his boys before having two little girls of her own.

After ten years passed since Jill gave birth to her son, all is now forgotten. Sometimes memories are a little like God's grace. People forgive and forget their transgressions and those who transgressed against them, and they continue with their lives. What was once the gossip of Warren is forgotten, and only Jill recalls the scandal when she was only sixteen years old.

Jill's episode of having a baby out of wedlock was a driving force as Dove and Penny decided to involve themselves with unwed mothers, and this spark ignited the flame in her heart that was instrumental in opening the Stevens Home for Unwed Mothers a few years later. Fortunately, over the years, families have mellowed and become more accepting of teenagers who make errors of judgment. There is much more willingness to forgive daughters and less severe negative social stigma generated towards single moms. Certainly, this is one of the better changes in American society over the years. Family love and unity is a better solution than denying and disowning daughters gone astray.

Chapter 33
Questions about Penny

D r. Jake Stevens was a family medical doctor practicing in Warren since 1930. He finished his residency at Johns Hopkins University, and began practicing medicine in a small western Pennsylvania town, in need of his surgery expertise. Jake was recruited by many leading cities where he would have much greater earning potential, but a belief he was born to serve prompted him to choose Warren, because of the town's desperate need, and the beauty of the area. Unlike doctors of more recent years, his practice covered every family need from internal medicine, obstetrics and child care to major surgery.

Jake knew his patients well, and he often made house calls when necessary because many people were denied medical attention due to the lack of transportation or income. Every Wednesday afternoon he returned home after his hospital work and took care to keep his skills honed, but he always tenderly remembered that day when Penny arrived at his door. Jake loved his work and his patients.

Penny grew up too fast to suit her parents, and when she left for Pennsylvania State University Jake and Lois were lonely and somewhat lost living in their large, white, riverfront house. They were overjoyed when they first met their son-in-law, and Dove became Jake's best friend in the ensuing years. Jake and Lois insisted their daughter bring her new husband to live in their house because the entire second floor was empty, and they relished the opportunity to have their daughter back home again.

Jake and Lois hoped Penny would have a baby, but they knew the chances were extremely slim, if not nonexistent after her miscarriage. Penny was busy with teaching school, and Dove was often traveling for his employer, along with researching for a novel, his photography, and his doctorate thesis. It was not a surprise they spent years waiting and hoping, only to be disappointed. Lois and Jake talked many times during the evening hours about the wonderful love between Dove and Penny, and what fabulous parents the couple would be. Their new hope was that they would soon adopt a child or two.

In late 1969, while attending a medical conference in Pittsburgh, Jake participated in a small group discussion about unwed mothers, back alley abortions and care for abandoned children whose young mothers were trapped in uncompromising families. The discussion addressed counseling pregnant teenagers with possible legal solutions for their dilemmas offering both support for women and homes for the babies.

During the discussion among several medical doctors, Jake told of his adult daughter, Penny, and how she had been deposited on his doorstep, so many years ago. Although Penny was the only baby left unannounced on his doorstep, he and his wife, Lois, had worked with unwed mothers and families of unwed mothers regularly to help them develop a plan to navigate the rough waters at home and school.

Only a few weeks after the conference, Dr. Larry Mead contacted Jake regarding a baby born in Franklin in the spring of 1943 who had disappeared and was never heard from again. The two doctors met for dinner one evening in Tionesta, a small town about halfway between Warren and the Franklin home of Dr. Mead. During their meeting, the two shared everything they knew about the baby from Franklin and Penny, now twenty-six years old. The dates of one child leaving Franklin so suddenly and another being abandoned in Warren made both doctors consider if they were the same baby.

Both doctors decided to gather any data they could uncover, and meet again if they detected any explicit details linking the babies together. Jake had mixed emotions about learning anything that would connect Penny to another family, but he was resolved to explore whatever information was gained.

Jake's resources in Warren to research Penny's possible birth parents were virtually non-existent, but his mind lingered on the possibility she might become close to another family if a connection was verified. Jake never shared his concerns with Lois, and he never discussed the meetings he had with Dr. Mead.

Nearly six months after the two doctors met for the first time in Tionesta, they met again to discuss Penny and the missing baby from Franklin. By now, Dr. Mead believed Penny, and the baby dropped at Jake's door were the same, but no birth record could be found in the hospital records. Dr. Mead had searched every accessible piece of data attempting to piece the segments together, and concluded that perhaps the child was born at home instead of in a hospital, but he could find no records of the event in either newspapers or court proceedings. Jake began to doubt Larry's recollection from nearly thirty years ago because no facts surfaced to verify his memory, and Jake's scientific training required more proof before action.

Dr. Mead said, "You can continue this process or withdraw from the researching activity, as you wish. It's up to you Jake." When they finished dinner, Jake confided he was concerned there were no valid reasons to uncover historical facts that could cause harm to Penny. That was the final time they discussed Penny or the baby that may have disappeared from Franklin about the time of Penny's birth. It was not the last time Dr. Stevens consternated, and wondered how he should address the issue. Jake thought, "Even if Larry's memory is correct, how can I find more data on the birth, and do I really want to find more information after all these years?"

Jake considered talking to Lois about his possible revelation regarding Penny, but day by day, he delayed researching. He finally realized no benefit would be gained by sharing Dr. Mead's belief, however, plausible. Dr. Stevens knew there was a mystery involving Penny, and if there was a secret, he was not going to be the person to uncover it and share anything hurtful with Penny or anyone else. The secret was safe with him.

Chapter 34
Remembering the Wedding

Penny returned to the chapel for more relief and comfort, realizing she had more remembering and thinking to do. Occasionally a student walked past her and proceeded forward to pray or view the marvelous gothic building. Earlier in the day, a service was held when the chapel was filled with students, faculty and staff, as an organ recital was presented by one of the music majors. She recalled the organ music for their wedding played by the music department chair, but she could no longer recall his name. After forty-six years, her memory is unsure of some details while others are crystal clear in her mind.

That gorgeous Saturday afternoon, he played *Jesu, the Joy of Man's Desiring* which was sung by a beautiful young, dark haired soprano, who was an Associate Professor of Voice. As Penny sat in the pew, she could almost hear the hymn ringing through the chapel as it did that remembered August day, the day Dove and she were married. She recalled several wedding marches were played as their friends and guests were seated, left side for her family and friends and right side for Dove's. The pews were filled, and silence overwhelmed the chapel. Penny's father took her in his arms and whispered in her ear, "I will always love you Penny, but now I must give you away." He lifted her veil and kissed her cheek and said, "Penny, it's your turn now."

The Reverend Dr. Ron Scott, Bobby Morris, the best man and Dove were waiting in front of the chapel on the right side when the processional began. The groomsmen and bridesmaids began walking down the aisle in pairs, followed by the maid of honor, lifelong neighbor and best friend Karen O'Hara. Then her little nephew, Craig Stevens, carrying the wedding rings on a soft satin apricot pillow was followed by Ginger, the little tow-headed flower girl, who gently threw flower pedals along the way. After the wedding party had completed their procession to the front, the attendees stood facing the oncoming bride as *Wagner's Wedding March* began and the guests stood and turned to see the radiant bride approach the alter.

The march seemed long with every eye glued on her. Penny recalled being thankful for the veil that lightly covered and hid her blushing face as she approached the most handsome man she had ever known, even to this day. He stood tall wearing his black tuxedo with all the adornments including a black bow tie and a wide cummerbund. He stretched out his hand as Rev. Ron Scott asked, "Who gives this woman to be married?" Penny's incredible father looked her in the eye and placed Penny's hand in Dove's hand as he said, "Her mother and I." His voice started to crack, but he regained his composure, finished his line, then he hurried to sit with Lois. He blotted the tears that had seeped from his eyes, and began to enjoy the ceremony. As the bride and groom stood hand in hand in front of a full chapel, Jared Parish, a tenor with a fabulous vocal range, brought tears to almost every eye as he sang *If.* Today, the words are particularly poignant as Penny reflected on one of Dove's and her happiest days. As in the touching song, Penny was thinking about being with Dove again, today, tomorrow and forever and she would love the opportunity to fly away with him. She loved the song and memorized every word — long ago.

After Penny and Dove exchanged wedding rings and placed the symbols of endless love on their fingers, they made their sacred pledges facing one another, holding their four hands together. Penny's wedding ring snuggled up against the scintillating, flawless, one carat diamond engagement ring Dove had recently given her. The jewel was mounted in a Tiffany setting on an eighteen karat yellow gold ring, perfectly matching the gold wedding band.

The ceremony was complete when Dove and Penny rose after taking communion, and Dr. Ron Scott formally introduced them as "my son and daughter-in-law, Mr. and Mrs. Jon Scott, whom I am incredibly proud." As Penny heard the introduction she thought, "What a great way to tell us that he approves of our marriage, and he loves us." Certainly it was a stressful day, but it could not have been better.

After reliving one of her life's most rewarding days, she realized the afternoon had passed quickly as the sun was now low in the sky creating those unique designs on the pews. Penny rose from the bench and noticed her handkerchief was damp when she returned it to her purse. Memories are so precious!

They say it takes a minute to find a special person,
an hour to appreciate them, a day to love them,
but then an entire life to forget them.

~Unknown Author

Penny found her special person, long, long ago.

Chapter 35
Mission for Unwed Mothers

Fall has arrived here in western PA, so splendid days like today will be few and far between until spring. The sky is colored in that beautiful deep blue that is characteristic as days grow shorter in the fall. Today as she sits in the tranquil chapel, it is a matchless time to remember Dove's and her accomplishments. Cutting to the chase, Penny provided the dream and Dove and her parents, Lois and Jake Stevens, made the vision happen with their financial support, fundraising resources and their many contacts supporting her aspiration.

After teaching in elementary school for four years, Penny was asked to move over to senior high school to teach anatomy and biology. This was when her desire to help pregnant girls and unwed mothers began. She had the desire to create a home for unwed mothers in Warren County. Penny had already seen too many teenage girls suffer the sting of rejection when they confessed their pregnancy. Even in the best of circumstances these young women were ostracized by society. They had made their bed, and now they must lie in it, according to many. Little did they know how seriously their quick pleasure could negatively affect their entire lives, and Penny wanted to help them move past their deplorable situation in life. One sad fact is that many of the same parents had made the same error in judgment, but through sheer luck, they avoided the consequences of an unwanted pregnancy.

Dove and Penny realized they were incredibly fortunate, particularly considering their starts in life. Certainly not every adopted child has a happy life with loving and compassionate parents. By 1970, they began planning for a home for unwed mothers and or troubled teens in Warren. With their careers taking an inordinate amount of their time, they were trying to determine how to promote the idea to the town fathers, or perhaps the county, and establish fundraising efforts to make it happen.

Beginning after New Year's Day in 1973, Dr. and Mrs. Stevens buttoned up their home and were spending their winters in Florida. Each spring they returned to Warren and continued their medical practice, but each year they intentionally reduced their hours and numbers of patients. At one time, Dove and Penny had hoped to purchase Jake's and Lois' home overlooking the water to raise their children, in what Penny called the old homestead. Unfortunately, after her miscarriage, the doctors explained Penny would never be able to carry another child. They were hurt, stunned and remorseful, but they knew they needed to accept the unchangeable and move on with their lives. Without children, Dove and Penny could not justify the large Steven's homestead for only the two of them.

Her brothers, Ron and Steve, had successful medical practices, and their children were already in high school. The brothers never planned to return to Warren, so neither was interested in the beautiful home overlooking the Conewango Creek.

Lois and Jake planned to retire fully in 1975, and resolved to live in Ft. Lauderdale, Florida and take up golf. Their children were raised, and Jake had helped bring a new surgeon and a general practitioner to Warren. He felt he was ready to enjoy retirement life, after more than forty years practicing medicine. Late in December 1974, her father called and asked if Dove and she were available to join them for dinner at the Conewango Club on Saturday night.

When Penny and Dove arrived, the Stevens were already seated with their lawyer friend, Frank Massa and his wife, Mary. Over dinner, they discussed Jake's upcoming retirement and dad announced he would help fund a home for unwed mothers, first by donating his home to establish a non-profit organization dedicated to the cause. Dove and Penny were taken completely by surprise because Jake and Lois never mentioned a plan to help Penny attain her greatest passion. They knew her parents were affluent, and their children were remarkably successful, but they had no idea the family house would be the bedrock for a foundation Penny so spiritually endorsed. Jake said, "Lois and I have been blessed with three healthy and successful children, none of whom need our financial help, and we feel very privileged to have served in Warren for many wonderful years. We feel the need to give something back to our town and the people here, and at the same time, we can support a program we know you are completely devoted."

As dinner progressed, Jake announced he and Lois would stay in Warren and offer their medical services free to unwed mothers at the new medical care center. The medical office in the front room of the donated house could be used to provide care for the residents. Jake would continue with obstetrics and child care, and Lois would be his nurse. Putting the frosting on the cake, he said, "Frank Massa had already agreed to provide free legal support for the foundation and the unwed mothers as required."

There was only one caveat. Penny was to be the first Executive Director, and accept full responsibility for assembling a team to provide services to continue educating the women, ensure they earned their High School Equivalency Diploma, and place them in the workplace after giving birth. Frank and Mary, because they had many prosperous clients with old money, also agreed to head the team to raise funds from the community.

Dove and Penny were astonished as they listened to Frank and Jake outline plans to implement the objectives to put the entire scheme in motion within six months. This was one of Penny's proudest moments, as she realized her hopes were being kick-started long before she thought possible. Penny always knew her parents had compassion for others, but this action proved their commitment to help others with the time and talent they had remaining.

Penny wanted to stay longer, but clouds were coming in from the west and the temperature was dropping rapidly, so once again she said a prayer for her mother and father, her brothers, and for her beloved Dovie before heading for the exit. She walked towards her car, pulling her collar up and buttoning the top button on her warm, furry jacket.

Once again, Penny thought of Dovie's favorite line: "Love is good," and she remembered how her family had plenty of love to share.

Chapter 36
Trudy Johnson – Beaten and Raped

Trudy Johnson was a blond haired, blue eyed eighth grader when she was carried into the hospital at 11:30PM on May 3, 1974. She was severely beaten with cuts on her face, arms and legs along with an obviously broken left arm. The ambulance delivered her to the emergency room after finding her lying in front of her home between the sidewalk and the street. Following the urgent call revealing her exact location on West Third Avenue, near the corner of Water Street, the medics found Trudy unconscious when they arrived. Wearing shredded shorty pajamas, the blood covered fourteen year old lay by the road after apparently crawling from her home to the street.

Dr. Jake Stevens was in the hospital waiting for a patient to deliver her fourth baby when the sirens alerted him an emergency existed, so he hurried to the ER to assist. When he saw Trudy he instantly recognized the little blond, even though her face and eyes were swollen. He recalled her name and remembered her mother, Violet Johnson. Jake had treated

Trudy's mother for spousal abuse after a severe beating at the hands of her husband, Frank. Spousal abuse was one of the most ubiquitous and disgusting parts of being a medical doctor, trying to repair broken bodies needlessly destroyed by a partner.

Immediately, Jake observed Trudy had been severely beaten as evidenced by the extensive contusions and lacerations on her arms, neck and legs. Additionally, her body was smeared with blood, especially on her arms and chest areas. As he cut away her pajamas, he saw bruise marks on her small breasts and severe discoloration of her abdomen. It was also visually apparent that Trudy had a badly fractured radius bone midway between the elbow and the wrist, and a cut lip along with a severely blackened left eye.

Setting the arm bone required sedation, and while she was unconscious the doctors noticed other deep bruises and scratches on her inner thighs and pubic area, which indicated rape. Dr. Stevens knew immediately that Trudy needed an x-ray before he could set the fracture, but only after cleaning her up and arresting the blood flow from her wounds. Before treating her wounds, Jake asked an assistant to photograph her injuries for the district attorney's help in prosecuting the offender.

Trudy's mother was divorced three years earlier after her husband's vicious attack left her with blackened eyes and severe abdominal blows that caused a miscarriage. Frank, her husband, was served with a warrant, charged with assault to commit murder, and served two years in the penitentiary for the beating. Violet was given court protection after his release from prison earlier this year, but Frank continued to harass Violet from time to time, particularly after nights of drinking, but she never reported the continued protection violations.

It was nearly 4AM Saturday morning before Trudy's radius bone was set, and her arm was placed in a cast. Dr. Stevens

137

stayed to support the emergency room team complete a comprehensive rape examination, and take the appropriate steps to avoid sexually transmitted diseases and the remote possibility of pregnancy. Trudy was then moved to a private room Dr. Stevens ordered when he admitted her to the hospital.

Neither the hospital or police were able to reach Violet that night, and the police issued a missing person's report immediately. Subsequent to knocking, without a response on the already opened door, two officers entered Violet's home after seeing blood on the front stairs and several bright lights in the house. With the history of physical abuse by the truculent Frank Johnson, he was the primary suspect for child abuse and possible kidnapping. An All Points Bulletin was generated and spread immediately to all law enforcement agencies throughout northwestern Pennsylvania and southern New York.

Violet and Trudy lived alone in a small apartment on West Third Street, near the bridge over the Conewango Creek. Violet worked as a spot welder in the production of transistor bases for Eltronics, a small privately held company in Warren. She was able to walk the mile to and from work each day and made sufficient money to support her daughter. They had no vehicle for transportation, and it was unknown at the time, whether or not they had relatives in the Warren area. Additional details remained to be obtained, but Jake persuaded the cops to hold off until morning with their questions, because Trudy was in severe shock and not able to communicate that night.

The police began a history check on the family to discover more background data as they tried to piece the sexual assault together with the missing person case. The next morning, Dr. Stevens called Penny to tell her about Trudy, and she instantly realized that Trudy had been one of her third grade students five years earlier. "Oh dad," Penny questioned, "is Trudy going to be all right? Are there any permanent injuries?" Her father said that her physical injuries would heal, but she had been violently raped and beaten severely, and that can result in lingering psychological issues that sometimes never fully recover. "Sometimes" Jake said, "rape victims suffer extreme feelings of shame and guilt, even though they are totally innocent victims of senseless, violent actions of sex crazed criminals."

Penny remembered Trudy and how she was a shy little girl, keeping pretty much to herself in school. "Dad," Penny said, "she was an average little girl in almost every way. Her grades, her appearance, her clothes and her participation in class were all normal, but her shyness and her lack of good friends was unusual for a little girl of nine years old. Trudy liked to be close to me when the class ventured outside for recess or on a field trip, but I really never gave it much thought."

Penny's recollection was that Trudy only listed her mother on her school registration paperwork; therefore, she was unsure who was Trudy's father. She wished she had paid more attention to the child's home life, but now it was too late. Penny kept shaking her head, thinking that if Frank was the culprit, then he must not be Trudy's father. Certainly a father would not rape his own fourteen year old daughter, would he? Well, she knew it wouldn't be the first time for incest between a father and his daughter, but Penny stopped herself from that train of thought. It was premature to blame anyone at this time.

Chapter 37
Frank and Violet Found Dead

Penny was at her mom's and dad's home with Dove when the police arrived at 10AM Saturday morning. Two of Warren's police officers introduced themselves and joined them for coffee in the kitchen. They were shocked to learn Violet, was found shortly after daybreak floating in the Conewango Creek, just above the small dam below the millrace. She had been shot in the upper abdomen and apparently dragged from a car and dropped in the water from the Third Street bridge. Blood was found on the bridge walkway and railing, but there were no witnesses reporting the incident. News was slow to develop, and there was nothing reported in the Saturday Warren Observer. WNAE and WRRN, Warren's radio stations reported the floating body and the location, but the name of the victim was not yet released and the place of death was not reported.

Warren was unaccustomed to murder, and this was an obvious murder. Not since Judge Wade was shot in the courthouse while sitting on the bench, could Penny recall a murder in her hometown. That infamous day Norman Moon shot the judge while Moon was being tried for failure to support his childless spouse. It was January 24, 1954, and many residents believed Moon's spouse had a close relationship with the judge.

Two other police officers camped out at the Warren General hospital waiting to interview Trudy, but she remained totally unresponsive with unfocused eyes, making no sounds whatsoever. An armed officer maintained a vigil at her door, protecting her from a possible attack from her rapist, the probable murderer of Violet. There was a complete lockdown until another body was found and identified floating in the Allegheny Reservoir, near the Kinzua Wolf Run Marina. Frank Johnson had two holes in his head. One single bullet entered behind his right ear and exited through his left eye. A stolen canoe was drifting about twenty-five feet from the body when they were discovered by a fisherman about 10AM.

The mystery ended as quickly as it began, leaving only a battered, orphaned teenager, in a private hospital room, dazed and apparently unaware of the latest news. Three days passed before Trudy finally snapped out of her lethargy and began to communicate with Dr. Stevens and the police officers. Her story was horrendous, when Trudy revealed watching her step-father shoot her mother when she attempted to help Trudy escape Frank's attack.

The maniacal man raping her kept shouting, "Your mother is a tramp. I am not your father. You were two years old before I ever met your trashy mother, and she turned my life into a living hell." Trudy continued, "I saw mom bleeding from her upper stomach area, but she continued her struggle to free me from Frank." Trudy stopped talking and cried as she shut her eyes as if to blink the unpleasant memory away, but she persevered stating, "Then as mom collapsed she raised her right arm one last time to strike Frank again. She took one final gasp and exhaled her last breath after closing her fist and striking Frank with what little strength remained as she collapsed noisily to the floor, in a puddle of her own blood. Then Frank continued to punish me. He kept hitting, pinching, biting and scratching me, grabbing any part of my body where he could inflict cruel pain." Tears flowed from her eyes as she covered her face, hoping for her heartbreaking nightmare to end, and a sweet, fresh life to begin.

Chapter 38
Plans for Trudy

Jake told Penny the story, and she was nearly hysterical that anyone could be so cruel to a little fourteen year old, first killing her mother and then raping and inflicting severe pain and possible disfigurement all over her little body. Dove was sitting at Penny's side and said, "Somehow Penny, we will develop a plan to help this child seize the opportunity to regain the life to which she is entitled. She deserves a complete reprieve from this horror." Dove was sensitive, more than most men she supposed, but also strong and forceful, and Penny knew he would help find a way to alleviate this teenager's extraordinary sorrow and pain. His fists were closed, and his teeth tightly clenched as he troubled over Trudy's affliction. "We can help her, don't you think, Penny?"

This episode was the first and only time when Dove and Penny experienced severe, violent actions, from anyone, and of course they were not actually involved. They were not experienced with lawless behavior, and thankfully, they never experienced anything like this again. Dove came to Penny that night wanting to put together an action plan to assure Trudy was rescued from this deplorable situation. They learned Violet was an only child whose mother resided in Tennessee, albeit in extremely poor health. "Dove," Penny asked, "how can we help this child and make a difference in her life?"

Dove and Penny talked to both sets of their parents seeking advice, only to receive their view that this was something they would have to determine for themselves. Finding a temporary foster home for Trudy was the first thing to consider as obviously, Trudy could not go home; home was no more, and she was alone in a town of fifteen thousand friendly people. Dove asked, "Penny, what would you think about volunteering to be Trudy's foster parents while she recovers from her terrible ordeal?" She knew her eyes must have nearly popped out of their sockets because she had not considered that option. Like most people, she was thinking someone else would step up to the plate and provide Trudy help. In the back of her mind, Penny continued to hope for a miracle, and that Dove and she would have their own baby, but she knew it was a dream that would probably never come true, but no one ever said she gave up easily.

Dove and Penny lived just two miles outside of Warren on their twenty acre gentleman's farm, and the neighbor children were bussed to the Warren schools. Penny guessed it would be a transition from living near the downtown area, but Trudy would love the wildlife and nature of country living. They had tried to garden, but the deer and rabbits devoured anything that grew, so they shopped for fruit and vegetables at Big Joe's Market in North Warren, and they photographed nature's four legged team of shrubbery pruners feasting on the succulents. Sometimes, they talked about getting a horse or two, but they reluctantly shied away from that idea as they knew it would restrict their other activities like hiking and canoeing. On the other hand, they had been thinking of a Shetland Sheepdog to help keep the deer at a safe distance from their plants. "Could this be the time for a puppy," Dove asked?

The Stevens were Penny's and Dove's sounding boards whenever they considered new life changing events, and like many other times, Dove and Penny invited them to dinner at the Savoy Restaurant, a mom and pop restaurant with delicious home cooking. The eatery served everything from hotdogs and hamburgers to roast beef, pork or turkey, and their "to die for" pie was the town's best dessert. The foursome selected a table where it was quiet, and Dove and Penny asked her parents what they thought about them adopting Trudy. Bless your hearts, Jake said, "I've been hoping that you would consider foster care or adoption for some time. We all know that having your own baby is extremely unlikely, but I know you would be marvelous parents, and you deserve to have the happiness that children offer." Then mom offered, "Having and raising children is difficult, but the rewards are fabulous. We had three children, and now we have six grandchildren and a great-grandchild is coming soon. The new generation is our life, now that we're about to retire."

"Do you think we could get Trudy?" I asked. "I have known her for several years," Penny continued. "She is a neat kid, one who would add joy to our lives, particularly after this trauma ends, and she moves on with her life." Dove chimed in, "From what I've heard, teenagers are much more difficult to place because many couples want a baby." Then her mom asked, "Will you be genuinely happy with a fourteen year old or would you rather try to adopt a baby? You need to determine that, Penny, before you make the decision with Dove." Penny loved the way her parents never told them what to do. They wanted them to consider all of their options and make the best decision for themselves. They were quick to support their

145

children's decisions but reluctant to influence them greatly. Is it any wonder they loved them? Many times Penny and Dove saw them retreat from attempting to control choices in their life. Perhaps that is one of the reasons they had such a fantastic relationship. Dove and Penny never felt they had to choose their parent's way; therefore, Penny and Dove took responsibility for their own decisions.

Returning home, Dove began his dictation session, recording his organized thoughts with vivid details, as the words just seemed to flow from his heart. Nothing nefarious was going to affect Trudy again as long as he could intervene. Each time he paused between thoughts Dove hesitated to develop the next, sequentially reviewing everything they knew about the sickening events. Then he outlined a plan to turn Trudy's regrets and despair into joy and a love of life. Could Dove and Penny make a difference in Trudy's life, or was she already so battered, ashamed and damaged that even love would not rescue her?

Chapter 39
Bringing Trudy Home

Trudy had remained in the Warren General Hospital for five additional nights before Dr. Stevens was ready to discharge her. She had many of the predictable emotional reactions women experience after suffering rape. She was often confused and sometimes lost control of her emotions and just began crying whether she was alone or with a visitor. She was afraid of the dark, and nervous when she was alone. She lost her appetite and rarely slept for more than a few minutes at a time. Dove and Penny were worried if Trudy had convalesced enough for them to take her into their home, but Trudy insisted with the county authorities she wanted to live with Dove and Penny, and she was ready to leave the hospital.

Penny's parents contributed immensely when Trudy came to live with Penny and Dove by staying overnight in the guest bedroom for the first three weeks. After the first week, Trudy asked, "Dr. Stevens, I'd really like to call you grandpa. Would that be all right with you?" Penny told Dove, "I wish you could have seen the tears stream down dad's face as he rushed to hug his new granddaughter." Jake said, "You can call me grandpa,

Trudy, I'd really like that, but I know someone who would like to have you call her grandma too. Would you like that?"

Penny believed that was the beginning of Trudy getting over the malaise following the violence perpetrated on her young body. It was not instantaneous, but it was the beginning of consigning her fear to the past, and remembering the nicest parts of her life. Yes, Trudy struggled with losing her mother, and sometimes she blamed herself for her mother's death, but day by day and week after week, she recuperated and became the child Dove and Penny never had. Trudy did not return to school that year, and Penny's summer vacation commenced three weeks after Trudy was discharged from the hospital. Summer vacation began, and choosing a new family dog was at the top of everyone's agenda.

Trudy and Dove searched for just the right puppy. They visited several breeders, but they could never locate the perfect little guy until they found Buddy, a three month old mahogany-sable sheltie. The kennel owners named him Ringer, but now he was Trudy's dog! Dove said, "Tru, I want you to name this little guy because he will become your constant companion and follow you wherever you lead." Tru looked up at him and said, "That sounds as he and I are going to be best friends, so I want his name to be Buddy!" He followed every move she made, rested by her chair wherever she sat, and slept on her bed at night. She had never owned a pet before, and the unconditional love given her by Buddy was instrumental in her recovery. Summer was sensational as the four of them became integrated as a family and lived a simple country life as God had intended, with love and joy.

Dove and Penny had an eventful summer helping Trudy conquer her sadness and depression. Penny worked around the house while Dove wrote most mornings until close to noon, and then they hiked and canoed or sometimes just took beautiful drives down the Allegheny River until they found a place to wet a line or have a delightful picnic. Trudy quickly learned their lifestyle, and she loved every minute together.

The memories of the spring savagery inflicted on Trudy faded by the time September rolled around, and thankfully, the despicable rape never made the news. When Trudy returned to school, her classmates thought she had endured a severe beating, but they knew her mother was murdered and that her step-father committed suicide. Penny planned to provide school transportation every day; however, Trudy expressed a preference to ride the bus and develop new friendships.

Dove and Penny had been married for nine years by the time Trudy became their foster child. Their careers had progressed wonderfully by then, and providing for Trudy was an opportunity to give something meaningful to one that deserved more. The immediate goal was to nurse Trudy back to perfect health, and love her as a naturally born daughter. Securely filling her life with happiness and the fullness of life that comes with being part of a family, was their longer term objective. Certainly, they planned for her to go on to college, but after that their aspirations became somewhat selfish, as Trudy would be their future and faithful friend and companion — just like any other parent hoped for their daughter.

The adoption process was facile. Trudy wanted Dove and Penny to be her parents, and they wanted her to be their daughter, much like Penny became her parent's daughter nearly thirty-two years earlier. What goes around, comes around! The county lawyers and judges made quick work of their petition, and Trudy Johnson became Miss Trudy Scott on March 22, 1975. The celebration marked a fortuitous day in Penny's and Dove's splendid lives, as less than one year after the horrific violent crimes perpetrated on Trudy and her mother, the adoption was finalized.

Chapter 40
Dove's Daughter

When Trudy came to live with Penny and Dove, the Scotts were her only viable option, and it was apparent she was happy to be with them. The first few months were stressful, mostly because of Trudy's anxiety and recurrent nightmares. Dove worried that Trudy would be standoffish towards him, after her experience with her step-father, but she soon began calling him "dad." That first summer Dove began calling her Tru, and when she saw her new father heading outside to work in the yard, she would say, "Dad, what can I do to help?" Mowing the lawn on the 19HP Wheel Horse tractor was her favorite job, and by the end of summer, she considered that chore to be her responsibility.

Tru liked to hike, fish and canoe, and by the second year Tru, Buddy and Dove often went exploring alone if Penny had other chores to accomplish. Her attitude became bubbly, and always positive, but she showed no interest in boys until her senior year in high school, Even then, she only occasionally went to a movie or a dance, and then she only double dated with another couple. One day while walking alone with Tru, Dove told her about Penny and him, and how they met overlooking Peyto Lake. Then he told her how they had already finished college before meeting, and that Penny was his only real girlfriend, the only girl he ever kissed. "And what's equally important," Dove told her, "is that I was her first boyfriend. Tru, when you find the right guy, you'll know; and if he's not the one, you will know that too. So, Tru, don't be impatient with love, it will come, just wait and see!"

One of the most exhilarating days was preparing Tru for the Senior Prom. She donned a pale yellow floor length satin gown with long sleeves and lace trim, and when Brian Davis, with a crimson face, pinned the red rose corsage on her, she looked like the fairy princess every girl dreams. Dove was convinced Penny was even more excited than Tru as the dress showed off the figure of a young woman, not the fourteen year old child they first knew.

"Can we go to the cottage?" Tru quizzed nearly every week during the summer. She seemed to love peace and solitude as much as Penny and Dove. Buddy loved the camp too, but because there were rattlesnakes in the deep forest, they always kept him on a short leash. By the end of summer, Buddy was nearly adult size, and his full, white collar, sturdy legs, tipped ears, narrow blaze and long, straight hair turned heads wherever they took him. If he had not been neutered, he could have been a fabulous show dog. Instead, Trudy trained Buddy as an obedience dog and often visited nursing homes with him. They used the cottage more in those four years than all the other years combined. Sometimes, Trudy brought a friend along, but more often she wanted to be alone with Buddy, Penny and Dove.

College was a concern for everyone. Trudy's grades were adequate, mostly B's with a few C's and an occasional A in the mix, but they never knew her career goals and aspirations.

When it came time to complete the applications, the three of them sat down over dinner to resolve two hugely important issues — what and where. "Mom and dad, I've been thinking about this for the past year or more, and I've decided to apply to Edinboro University and become a grade school teacher." "Trudy," Penny responded, "I didn't know you were considering a teaching career. When did you come to that decision and how did you settle on Edinboro?" Their precious daughter smiled and said, "Edinboro, because it's close and they have a great academic teacher program. I want to be able to come home often, so I considered Edinboro as my first selection. Also, some of my friends are planning to apply there too." Dove asked, "What friends, Tru?" As her face reddened, she replied, "Well dad, if you must know, Brian Davis! Brian has already applied, he's a good student, and I'm sure he will be accepted." Dove responded, "Those are good enough reasons for me, what about you Penny?"

When Tru went to college, the house became quiet again. The phone seemed out of order, for the constant ringing ceased with her absence. Buddy was lonesome for his master and watched for her return. On the first Saturday of every month, Penny and Dove traveled to Edinboro, a small town south of Erie, only 66 miles away from Warren. Once a month she returned home for the weekend to keep in touch with her friends, and keep her parents current with her young life. They were incredibly proud of Tru, particularly the way she recovered from her assault four years earlier.

Graduation day was a real thrill for the Scott family. With all the pomp and circumstance, Dove and Penny were beaming from ear to ear when Trudy crossed the stage and accepted her degree and teaching certificate that qualified her to teach grade school. Brian was right behind her by about thirty students, as he acquired his credentials to teach junior high school

152

mathematics. They were engaged on Christmas Eve of their senior year, and married on the second Saturday in June.

They teach in Titusville, PA, a small town about halfway between Warren and Grove City, so they are always close. They bought a small, tired old farmhouse on forty acres, much like the Scott home in Warren, and they've always had a sheltie to herd their kids, and now, their grandchildren. Brian is more adept at building and remodeling than Dove, but sometimes when they visit their daughter and son-in law, Brian allows Dove to assist around the farm; but Trudy still cares for the flowers, the trees and the lawn. What an enjoyable family time when everyone gets together to survey God's beautiful kingdom, walking quiet trails or floating down a lazy river. Penny and Dove followed their parent's tact, and allowed Tru to make her own decisions, and as the years passed, her decisions were usually wise.

Chapter 41
Dove's Mom

Growing up a preacher's kid in western Pennsylvania, Dove found his mother's interests were always different from his. Laura Stevens had more friends and was involved in more church projects than Dove's father, but in his defense, people were forever making appointments with him about church business, marriages, funerals, new member training, and other special programs. Mom, on the other hand, volunteered for four hours in a soup kitchen three days every week. She was the one who coordinated the coffee and treats in the narthex after church each Sunday morning, and too often she spent her Saturdays preparing the cookies, breads and fruit plates. Sometimes Dove would say, "Mom, why do you always have to provide the goodies, there are hundreds of ladies who never bring anything." She kindly responded, "I enjoy baking and it's an important job someone needs to do each week, Dovie. Many of these women work all week and don't have the spare time; some have little kids, some can't afford to provide the treats, and many are older women who have provided the treats for many years."

His little sister, Jenny, was completely different from Dove. She loved to hang out with her mother and help her cook and bake in the kitchen, while Dove was much more interested in his father's endeavors. Hiking, fishing, football and baseball were his favorite pastimes, and those were the activities his dad liked too. Jenny and Dove weren't very close, but they defended one another all through their childhoods. Perhaps the age difference was too sizable for them to be devoted friends when growing up, but as adults, they have grown close and sometimes they vacation together with their spouses.

When Dove was a child, Laura Scott was continually sitting in her favorite chair knitting or sewing items for someone she barely knew, or equally often, as a contribution for a fund raiser. Besides that, his mother entertained church ladies at the manse for a luncheon one day each week when she wasn't working at the soup kitchen. She was an extremely busy woman, fully invested in her life as a pastor's wife.

Dove recalled he was nearing twelve years old before he started to seriously appreciate his mother, and all the behind the scenes work she did for others. His father took Dove fishing, but his mother packed the lunches and fried the catch. His dad took him to ball games while his mom washed and ironed Dove's uniforms. Rev. Scott preached the sermon, but Laura stood beside him in the narthex, greeting every member and visitor. Dove thought many people saw his mother as just a "stay at home mom," but he knew different.

Once when telling Penny about his mother Dove said, "She was like the wheels that made everything move in my life, and now that I'm an adult, I understand how important she was in my life while I was growing up. She was also key to father's success as a preacher for nearly forty years. Dad was the pastor, but mother was the inspiration in his life, the person who understood the congregation's needs and communicated that knowledge to dad; and that is what made him such an excellent pastor."

Dove continued, "Dad practiced his sermons and rarely used a note as he left the podium after reading the scripture lesson, and he preached from the center of the platform in front of the altar table while he delivered a fifteen to twenty minute message to two hundred or more people each Sunday. I think dad was an outstanding preacher, always great with inspirational words about how to be a Christian. Mom lived the Christian life, caring for others her whole life. She did not wear her religion on her sleeve or around her neck; it kindled within her heart as she lived the life her husband taught. You could count on mom to teach the little girls in Sunday School, and to shepherd a women's Bible study in our home on Tuesday evenings. Usually, when I asked if I could help her, she would say, 'No Dovie, just run along and play. I can handle this.' I felt inadequate when I compared myself to mom. She toiled many onerous hours every day, but she loved to take on responsibilities and see them through to completion."

Later in Dove's teens and college years, his mother was on the sidelines with his dad for every sporting event. She encouraged him to find a career that satisfied his innermost desires. She counseled, "Dove, if you want to be truly successful in life, you need to love your work, love your family and love your God. When you have these triumphs in your life, many more wonderful characteristics follow like integrity, compassion, charity, wisdom and respect." When Penny heard Dove talk of his mother, she gained new respect for both Dove and his mother and thought, "I'd like someone to say something that respectful about me someday."

156

When Penny and Scott called and told his mom about Trudy, Dr. Scott was away on a church pastor's retreat. Laura said, "I think adopting Trudy is a fantastic opportunity for you, one that gives you an opportunity to love your own child, just like I love you, Dovie." Dove was surprised when he heard those words from her, because she was a private person, not one to spill her love outwardly. She continued, "You will find great pleasure watching this little girl blossom and become a witness to your goodness as you and Penny share your lives with her. The real joy is in the results you achieve."

Mom and Trudy became closer than Dove expected, after all, his mother didn't live down the street, but nearly two hours by car. He knew girls were special to her, and he knew they would have been closer had he been a girl like Jenny. Dove's mother made clothes for Trudy and taught her how to sew and knit. Laura loved to accompany Tru shopping for the latest teenage fashions; and it was his mother who taught Trudy to bake and cook, just like she taught her daughter, Jenny, to be one of the finest cooks he has ever known.

Whenever Penny and Dove went away for a long weekend, his mother came to stay with Trudy, and they became consummate companions, as did Buddy, for mom never had a pet in her home. Mom stated, "When dad retires and we have more time, I want a dog, just like Buddy." I thought to myself, "Mom, you will never retire from all the activities you volunteer; that is your life, that is who you are: someone who gives and gives and gives some more!" Still, a puppy would be a fabulous retirement present, a gift that would give her great pleasure in return for the joy she provided others. Yes, mom deserves a dog!

Chapter 42
First Years in Grove City

When Dove and Penny moved to Grove City in 1980 because of his new position as a professor there, they sold their home in Warren but kept the little cottage located deep in the Allegheny National Forest. It was really a simple little place about a mile off a secondary road near Heart's Content. They never spent the time there they had hoped when they purchased the place with over one hundred acres of beautiful hardwood forest and a stream with hungry native trout.

Often they spent the first weekend of trout season at the two bedroom cottage, but their many other commitments prohibited them from using the property often. They had a stream flowing past the little red cabin without electricity, so they kept their food supplies in a large crock with a heavy lid that was placed directly in the stream. Milk, eggs, hot dogs, hamburger, butter and bacon were kept fresh and secure from wild animals like raccoons. Generally the meat was packed back in the pick-up truck on Sunday before sunset if they were successful with their fly rods. Both of them loved trout and often had it for breakfast with eggs and corn meal mush after fishing at sunrise for a couple of hours.

Once Penny and Dove were in Grove City, they decided to begin a sister home for unwed mothers in the small, serene village of about 8,500 people, including students. This endeavor was much easier to establish because they had more knowledge of state and local laws, and they had been able to find people willing to assist them as her parents did a decade earlier. Dove had become a famous and prolific author and thanks to his kindheartedness, financial matters were resolved quickly.

Grove City, being home to a college filled with young people would be a challenge in some ways, but exceptionally rewarding in others. Considering the number of young unmarried women, the statistics indicated birth control had succeeded dramatically in the last ten years. "The Pill" was accessible to those who were sexually active, but many, if not most, of these young people at Grove City College were chaste, and abstained from sex until after marriage. Most of the outreach was to high school girls, just as they experienced in Warren.

Dove had published fourteen fabulously successful novels by 1980 and he was one of America's best known authors. The remuneration from the sales of books allowed them to contribute significant cash to the unwed mothers charity each year. As Dove's popularity as an author surged, he was often invited to college retreats or as a special guest speaker, and he accepted whenever he could.

One Thursday, Penny was able to accompany Dove to Rochester, NY where he spoke in chapel the following morning at Roberts Wesleyan College, a small liberal arts college with a growing reputation among Christian colleges. Penny believed it was there she realized Dove's gift for public speaking. He captured the imagination of the entire student body with his aureate language in Roberts' new Hale Auditorium when his topic was: *It's Your Life, Start Your Legacy Now!* Her pride was nearly sinful as she stood beside this pillar of a man and greeted the many students and professors gathered in the lobby to thank him for the majestical message.

After a meeting with the college administration and having a nice lunch at Garlock Commons, Dove and Penny continued to Letchworth State Park to photograph the blazing color of fall along the northward flowing Genesee River, as it snaked towards Lake Ontario. Dove retained his enthusiasm for photography and continued to improve his skills and stay abreast of the available equipment. They stayed at a quaint inn, the Glen Iris, which consistently offered some of the best food they encountered on their many weekend trips. The river carved a gorge nearly 600 feet deep through rock as the water rushed under an old railroad trestle bridge, and then gushed over three major waterfalls as it searched for lower terrain as it flowed to Lake Ontario. Penny and Dove joined a white water rafting excursion on the river on Saturday morning and then hiked the canyon, often referred to as the Grand Canyon of the East. Packing up the car, Dove commented he would like to come again to visit Eastman Kodak's giant manufacturing plant and stop at Roberts to learn more of its founder, B. T. Roberts, and the development of the college. He was thinking of another novel he had in the works. They headed home on Sunday morning, marveling at the scenic wonderland as they headed west along I-86 towards Salamanca, NY. They took a backroad shortcut up over the hill past the Allegheny Reservoir, through Scandia, past the Dove stone quarry high on the hill, and down into Warren before heading back home to Grove City. It was a shortcut her dad showed Penny many years ago. What a great weekend!

Chapter 43
Dove Learns the Secret

Dove's career was all he had ever dreamed. His formal education reached a new high when he earned his PhD in Comparative Literature from Cornell University in 1969; but joining Grove City College in 1980 as Assistant Professor of English Literature and Creative Writing was paramount in his professional life. Dove had easily advanced through graduate school as a freelance writer and photographer for several magazines, and in late 1970, he published his first historical novel depicting military life and love in America during the Cold War. *At the Ready* was propelled to the NY Times Best Sellers List in 1971 increasing his popularity and demand as a literary speaker nationwide, particularly on the university circuit.

Penny was also successful with her teaching career while providing incredible support as Dove became a prominent name in the literary world. She had earned a master's degree in education, but declined advancement to administrative positions on more than one occasion because of her desire to teach and maintain contact with students. She did move to senior high school where she taught classes in biology and anatomy beginning in 1970, after she earned her advanced degree. Her focus outside school was teenage pregnancy and helping prevent dysfunctional life following these crises.

The couple had been married for fifteen years when Dove was tapped for his position at Grove City College, and by then, Trudy was already finishing her second year at Edinboro University. It was evident they would never have their own children, but Trudy was a fabulous substitute. Because of her natural aptitude with children, Penny exhibited all the traits to be an excellent mother to any child. Certainly it was not for lack of trying that the couple remained childless, as both loved with the same intensity as when they first married, but they had known from that dreadful night when she lost their baby, she would never conceive again. Nevertheless, after recovering from their grief and sadness, their moods were always positive and they were so thankful for the many God given talents they possessed.

Penny retained her petite stature, weighing in at her same one hundred-five pounds since senior high school. Dove was still fit, but continuous traveling, dining out and less time for exercise and hiking had taken a toll on his broad shoulders and narrow waist; still, he was a handsome man that caused heads to turn.

Dove never had an interest in genealogy until Penny and he took up residence in Grove City. He was not focused on his birth family, but he started poking around different libraries and historical associations in 1991, as time permitted. Dove was fifty years old, and a fully tenured professor at Grove City College. He obviously knew where he resided as a child and started to search in Franklin, the first place he lived with his mother and father. Both of his adoptive parents had passed away before Dove had any interest in genealogy, and he regretted that he never attempted to learn more about his birth parents from them.

Partly because Dove was now quite famous, he was recognized at once by the library's staff in Franklin after he successfully obtained information for a novel. While making copies, the head librarian approached Dove and struck up a conversation. As they chatted, he disclosed his interest to delve into his genealogy, and she volunteered to begin the search for him. Mary Robbins loved Dove's novels, was enamored with his genius and was more than pleased to forage the library's many historical books, as well as census data, to get him started. Dove told her the little he knew, and Mary Robbins took it from there.

Within a month, Mary, the sixty something year old widow, phoned Dove to set up an appointment to discuss her findings. Not only had the gray haired, compassionate woman discovered more about his birth father; she had learned about others in his family and gave him copies of the records she had discovered. Of course, Dove always knew he was adopted, but he never knew the last name of his father. He had never cared before, but knowing he was born Jon Davidson was exciting.

Mary saw the pain in his face as he riffled through the paperwork and how he dwelled on every record. But Mary didn't fully comprehend what caused the strange look in his eyes and his flushed face or the laborious breathing that commenced. Tears started to reservoir in his eyes before freely streaming down his face and soaking his freshly pressed, short-sleeved dress shirt. Mary knew more, but she decided to withhold additional information until he was more settled. Quickly, Dove thanked Mary, slid his chair away from their table, stood and exited with the files as rapidly as possible.

Being a writer in need of detail, Dove started a search that resulted in untold pain. Once he knew the last name, Davidson, learning about his father's death was easy. Jon Davidson was a World War ll hero who, like so many other soldiers, died at the bloody battle of Tarawa along with nearly 3,000 Marines and 4,700 Japanese soldiers. He was one of thousands slaughtered trying to make landfall. When the four day battle was over, Jon Davidson was dead, the Americans had taken the island, and only seventeen Japanese survived the invasion.

Jon's father made the front page of the Oil City Derrick on December 1, 1943, more than a week after the battle of terror was over. Most of the Americans who died never made landfall from the landing craft. The razor sharp coral and the imbedded Japanese soldiers cut down the Americans when they were moving from the landing craft to the shoreline in about three or four feet of water. Jon never made shore alive, but the following day he washed ashore.

Within another month, Dove had uncovered enough family history to shake his very existence. He had uncovered a secret he could never share. Dove had a sister he never knew existed, and it was apparent his wife, Penny was his sister. They had the same parents! As Dove considered his options, he realized some of life's mysteries are best left unsolved. "Everyone has secrets," he thought, "every couple holds secrets from one another. As open as Penny and he were with one another, we have privacy, and we don't always share every detail of every event in our lives." Dove always believed some things are better left unsaid. People don't intend to rationalize, but one never tells a lady that her dress is ugly!

"Oh, Jonathan," he wailed to himself, that's what his mother used to call Dove when she was really serious and expected prompt action, "how can you withhold this secret from Penny? This isn't some trivial matter that is insignificant in the greater canvas of your life. This affects Penny too, just as much as me."

Dove was worried, incredibly worried, that his attraction for Penny would change. Could his love change from best fiend and lover to the non-sensual love of a brother for his sister? "What if I can't treat her like a wife? What if I can't perform as her husband, now that I know she's my sister," Dove worried. He struggled with these questions for hours before ever returning home that first evening.

He realized he couldn't share this discovery with Penny and break her precious heart, just as his heart was already crushed. He was only fifty years old and not willing to become a celibate partner anymore than he was prepared to endure a life without Penny. He worried that Penny would sense something was amiss, and demand answers to his new demeanor; but thankfully their relationship never changed, and Penny never challenged the new Dove, the man who loved his sister! Yes, there were days when he was somewhat languid, despondent and remorseful, but he recognized he needed to make a special effort to hide his feelings. He felt penitent and feared she would detect he was concealing a lie. Obviously, he hid their genealogy because he loved Penny intensely, but also to prevent his happiness from evaporating because of her rejection.

Fortunately, Dove triumphed over his stress by committing more hours to writing and more time at the college, but, he never once considered sharing his secret with Penny after the first month of constant mental anguish. Penny was his wife, and he, her proud husband. They committed before God, friends and relatives to eternal vows, and he would never seek release from God or his Penny! Dove knew he could never thank God enough for helping him through those protracted weeks of turmoil, doubt and fear.

Dove knew he could never bring himself to share his new found knowledge with Penny, leaving himself with a secret he could never divulge to a single person. The more Dove thought about his dilemma, the more he realized he needed a method of relieving the oppressive tension deep within his mind. Finally, he knew the answer. He would write a novel to be published only after his death. Keeping the data secret would not be difficult, therefore, in 1992 he began a computer file named *The Secret Never Shared* on his new Macintosh computer.

Chapter 44
Who You Are

Dove and Penny occasionally discussed their favorite quotes over dinner after a full day's work. Dove loved to quote Ralph Waldo Emerson, particularly, "Who you are speaks so loudly I can't hear what you're saying." Penny had never heard the quote until Dove introduced her to the line, but she had to admit it became one of her favorites. One day at school she discussed this quote from the great transcendentalist because two or three bright kids were failing her class. These boys were not failing because they were slow, they were failing because they were not reading their assignments or doing their homework. She also knew that they were failing some other classes.

One day, in order to get the conversation started, Penny asked the class if they had any career plans. There were always a few who liked to speak up, and sure enough, she heard plans to be a doctor from one particularly bright boy. She asked him why he wanted to be a physician, and he had several notable answers that brought everyone into the conversation. "I want to open a practice, so I can help people live a longer and healthier life, but I also want to have a profession that will allow me to provide a wonderful life for my family."

One tall, athletically inclined girl said she wanted to be a gym teacher, and another girl said she planned to take over the family farm and have a large family. Of course, that caused an uproar. The failing boys didn't have anything to volunteer, so finally Penny called on Johnny, one of the best liked boys in his sophomore class. "Tell me Johnny, what do you think you will do with your life," she asked? "Well, Mrs. Scott, I haven't thought much about it yet," he answered.

After another question or two, he said he also wanted to have a large family and have a job that would allow him to travel the world. From that point, the conversation was easy, and he admitted that he needed to start taking responsibility for his life and preparing for his future. Both other boys, who were failing, soon agreed they needed to pass their classes, graduate and live a life commensurate to the one their parents provided for them.

Too many youngsters claim they want one thing in life, but their actions tell the world they're not serious. It's a little like the young lady who says she wants to be a nun, but chases any boy wearing pants. Teenagers are dreamers, They dream of happy times, loving spouses and exciting jobs making tons of money, but too often they never prepare themselves to satisfy life's prerequisites for their success, and the fulfillment of their dreams.

Days like that didn't happen often, but they provided the reason Penny loved to teach. This lesson in life had nothing to do with tests or knowledge of biology, but these three boys changed their outlook on school, and they recognized their whole life depended on how they prepared while in school. All three graduated from high school, and two went on to finish college and became teachers.

Chapter 45
Regrets

Dove felt incompetent when he feared he was unable to father a child. Many of their friends were asking, "When?" And when Penny lost their baby, he wondered if the fault was actually his. Could he be unable to create life? Would Dove ever recover from knowing he would never be able to father a child with Penny? His mental anguish distracted him from concentrating on his writing, and the despair separated him from Penny for many weeks. Excluding the heartbreak of losing their baby and learning Penny could never conceive again, regrets were few in Dove's lifetime, until that fateful day Mary Robbins shocked him with news of the genealogy research she shared with him in 1991.

Dove was in a state of shock when he expeditiously excused himself and fled the library, but there was no escaping his newly learned knowledge. After waiting an excruciating week, Dove called Mrs. Robbins and returned to gather the remaining data she had devotedly gathered for him, and apologize for his abrupt departure. She understood his pain, and confided that the information she had gathered was confidential, and she would honor his right of privacy. Dove departed the library feeling relieved to know that the decision to retain or share the newly discovered data was his.

Dove's life changed dramatically when he first learned that Penny, the love of his life, was undoubtedly his sister. First, he was in denial, and he refused to accept the evidence as valid. The main reason Dove's life became so troubled, was his resolve to keep secret all the troubling information he received from Penny. He worried how and where he could save Penny from ever learning about their relationship, much like an adulterer keeps his infidelity secret. This decision prevented Dove from seeking anyone to help him through his agony. The longer he kept the secret, the more ashamed Dove became, and the more difficult to be the loving compassionate husband he had always promised.

Dove could never talk about his birth mother and father or grandparents, and he could never take Penny to the cemetery where they were buried. Shame became a part of his life, not because he took his sister as his wife, but because he was being deceitful to the woman he loved, even more than life itself. Dove's college workdays increased to relieve him from facing Penny. He was dreadfully unhappy and developed some novel characters to shunt his pain in a different direction. The longer he hid his secret, the more secretive he became; and the more secretive he became, the more he feared losing Penny.

Everyone has regrets of some variety, but Dove realized this was a circumstance he did not cause, and for which he was not responsible. Yet Dove understood he was withholding information from Penny because he feared she would terminate their marriage, and if she didn't, the legal system might! "I must get this nightmare out of my mind and move along with my life, I cannot undue this any more than I can turn back a calendar or unwind a watch."

As people move from one stage of their lives to another, the same stimuli affect them differently. Dove always believed that people passed through three stages in life. First, a learning stage where people search for their calling in life, and educationally prepare for a doing stage. The doing stage is when an individual takes the knowledge learned and applies it to a career, hopefully for the betterment of the world. Later in life, people enter the teaching stage where they assist others to take their place as doers. When people are young they can easily delay completing their goals until later, but as they age, the windows of opportunity close and they can never accomplish some tasks that require prerequisites. It's the learning and doing stages that can never be retrieved. "Here I am, in the doing stage of my life, and I don't have the answers," Dove thought. "How can I resolve this wisely? What would Solomon do?"

Dove considered the woman who wanted to have children and faced a time certain in her life when the opportunity is gone forever. The regrets people have occur after their moment has passed, when there is no time for another chance, or as they say in golf, "a mulligan." Whether the regret is failure to forgive someone before the opportunity is gone, or not marrying a loved individual because you want something that person cannot provide, Dove felt the pain.

Dove would be untruthful if he said, "I have no regrets other than my genealogy," because both Penny and he grieved when they lost their baby. Nevertheless, they seized the moment when Trudy came into their lives. They always hoped and prayed that God would provide a bundle of joy for them to love, nurture and teach. People need to pray and let God provide the solution, but prayers sometimes are answered in

171

ways people never expect. They wait to hear a response from God that is exactly as they planed, but not like God provided. Had Penny and Dove declined to adopt Trudy, their prayer would have been answered, but they would never have claimed it, and then they would have regretted the decision — and blamed God.

God answers prayer perfectly. He prevented a child who may have had severe health issues due to the fact that unknowingly, Penny and Dove were siblings. God provided a healthy child, who supplied the love of a daughter, the joy from grandchildren and now, the pride of having great-grandchildren with exciting futures. What more could anyone ask? One of Dove's novels reports, "Giving up control is one of life's hardest lessons to learn. We want to do everything our way, the way we are comfortable or the way we were taught. We also want our prayers answered the exact way we planned." For Dove, it was exceedingly hard not to recognize God answered their prayers.

He continued, "Too often, parents and teachers have control issues over mundane situations that can ruin relationships. Whether it's chewing gum or the length of someone's hair, that should not be the issue. We should agree that noisy chewing and dirty tousled hair are unacceptable. That's not to say no control is good, but reasonableness needs to be used to compromise and remove feelings of hate or disrespect."

Dove wrote, "I am reminded of a gifted teenage son who wanted an unlimited curfew on Friday and Saturday nights." The father asked his son, "Why do you want an unlimited curfew?" The son replied, "Dad, all of my friends have an unlimited curfew, and I feel weird with my 10:30 curfew when all the other guys can stay out as late as they choose." The father responded, "young man, you may have an unlimited curfew, but if you come home after midnight, I'll rescind it, and you will go back to your 10:30 curfew after your one month grounding period is complete." The teenager was thrilled with the compromise and never once violated his unlimited curfew.

Dove believed, "The best way to avoid regrets is to accept the unchangeable and compromise your desires to an achievable goal. We can't all live in a mansion and marry a prince or princess, but there are many other wonderful people and affordable houses which might be turned into great homes with wonderful and loving lives within. The important possessions in life are our families, friends and health, and they can all flee from us when we neglect them."

Dove never shared his secret with Penny, and he continued to dread the day she learned about his fears, or she learned he prevented her from knowing something she had a right to know. Dove supposed he was controlling Penny because he feared her response. That's where his shame remained, and that is his biggest regret. He would like to beg her forgiveness and retrieve his pride, but he is too afraid of losing her forever! When she reads this in his computer file notes, she will understand and forgive his selfishness and protectiveness, but for now, the shame Dove feels for denying her the right to know their relationship haunts him, and he worries that one day when she reads hidden computer files she will rethink her love for him! Dove hopes not!

Chapter 46
Dove's Death

It was totally unexpected! Both Dove and Penny were physically fit, with the typical aches and pains for people their age. Dove turned seventy on May 17, 2011, and Penny was two years behind him. Their serious hiking was long past, but they often took leisurely walks around the Grove City College campus or in Warren when they visited there. On warm, sunny days they often went to Cook Forest, which is about an hour east of Grove City, to fish, walk the beautiful trails or sometimes just to sit and watch wildlife.

Dove had his annual physical in May, and he was declared fit, as usual. His cardiologist ordered a stress test and a complete physical every year to follow up with the high blood pressure and diabetes discovered years earlier. As always, Dr. Eberly ordered a complete battery of blood tests including a PSA test to check for prostate cancer. All reports looked normal to his doctor, yet Dove died instantly while walking hand in hand with Penny in Cook Forest. He never made a noise; he just collapsed to the ground like a felled tree, and he never moved again.

Penny dropped to the ground and cradled Dove's head on her lap and searched for a pulse from his carotid artery, as she placed her other hand on his heart, but silence prevailed. The beat was gone, his breath was still, and his eyes were forever closed. There was nothing Penny could offer to help her lover of forty-six years and nothing that could help her either. Her breathing became labored as she gasped for oxygen to feed her dazed mind and sniveling body.

The EMS truck followed by a small fire truck arrived within ten minutes, but the autopsy indicated nothing could have saved him, even if this occurred in a hospital. Dove had a fatal aortic aneurysm which ruptured prior to the first symptom of physical discomfort. Penny realized only God can provide assurances about their lives, and Dove's life was in His hands. There was no doubt in her mind, as Penny watched him crumple in a heap below her that she would never be able to talk with Dovie again. She would never be able to love more than his memory or kiss more than his photo, but Penny's love for Dove was powerful with the sustaining support from all the books he authored and discussed with her over the years.

Penny thought of Shakespeare's famous line in Romeo and Juliet:

When he shall die,
Take him and cut him out in little stars,
And he will make the face of heaven so fine
That all the world will be in love with night
And pay no worship to the garish sun.

Now, Penny must accept her loss, just as she accepted her greatest find. Penny knew she would never be alone because her faith assured her that Dove and she will joyfully be together eternally in days that follow her grief.

175

Chapter 47
The Interment

Penny needs to get past some of the hardest parts of losing the love of her life. She struggles to remain positive, but the memories of Dove dwell deep within her mind, and there is no joy or pleasure at the moment. She is, once again, sitting in the chapel thinking about Dove's committal, for she knows she must critique all of the happy moments they shared together. She recognized that she soon forgets unpleasant experiences, but she retains delightful moments forever. Penny believes human minds categorize their memories into drawers that open easily and often to recall happiness; but they open infrequently to evoke sadness and tragedy, and that allows people to move along and continue to experience life.

The morning of the interment was dark and dreary when Penny opened the blinds, but the clouds parted and the beautiful uplifting sun broke through and started to warm the earth. She dressed in black as she prepared to go to the commitment and place the first dirt on his cold casket. Penny's eyes were swollen from crying herself asleep and loathing the day ahead. Three days she stood by Dovie's brushed bronze coffin and listened to friends, relatives, faculty and students pay their final respects and offer words of solace. The compassion was heartening, but there was no comfort in her heart. Thankfully, Trudy and her entire family, along with her nieces and nephews helped her through each day as she greeted the hundreds of mourners, and they kindly spelled her on occasion when Penny could stand no longer.

She thinks of Trudy, heartbroken at the loss of her father. Dove was her guiding light, the one she trusted unconditionally. Brian and the children knew Dove was the family's rock, and the one everyone expected to know the correct answer for any situation. Penny was confident in Brian and Trudy to pick up the pieces and march onward and upward though the path may be winding and steep.

Today, there would be a private burial with only a short message by the pastor before the burial. Dove was buried in the Oakland Cemetery in a plot overlooking the Allegheny River which they owned for many years. Certainly it was a peaceful place with a massive sugar maple shading the entire resting plot. Penny remembered walking through the exact area with Dovie saying, "When we're gone we can lie here beneath this massive maple tree, and watch and hear the river carry its water as it hurries towards the sea; and your favorite little town will always be in view under our watchful eyes."

Later a memorial service will be held in the Grove City College chapel when some of Dove's favorite music will be played in his memory. Penny's thoughts returned to the house where she was the little gift that was left on the stoop. God's Grace provided for her that cold spring day. A large, warm house with glorious memories of a lifetime was now the Stevens Home. Penny's mother was gone. Her father was gone, Ron and Laura Scott were gone, her brothers were gone, and now her beloved Dovie was gone too, leaving Penny alone with only her memories.

Then, Penny stood and tuned towards the grave, and she recalled Mary Frye's, *Do Not Stand at My Grave and Weep.* Could Dovie see her weep?

> *Do not stand at my grave and weep,*
> *I am not there, I do not sleep.*
> *I am a thousand winds that blow.*
> *I am the diamond glint on snow.*
> *I am the sunlight on ripened grain.*
> *I am the gentle autumn rain.*
> *When you wake in the morning hush,*
> *I am the swift, uplifting rush*
> *Of quiet birds in circling flight.*
> *I am the soft starlight at night.*
> *Do not stand at my grave and weep.*
> *I am not there, I do not sleep.*
> *Do not stand at my grave and cry.*
> *I am not there, I did not die!*

Chapter 48
Reflections of Dove

The chapel was abuzz this morning because the Grove City Football team was still undefeated after ten games. Dove would have been excited, for he fully supported all sports and music programs at Grove City College. He was a professor who seldom missed a college event, including attending many of the recitals performed each semester by the junior and senior students.

The undergraduates knew of his support, for each year he was the chapel speaker at least one time. True, his messages generally revolved around some ethical question in literature, often in his latest novel, but he always communicated his involvement with students, and in turn, they loved Dove to the point his classes were always overflowing. Three graduating classes dedicated their yearbook to him, and each time he was humbled by their deep affection. In addition to his classroom duties, while a professor at GCC, Dove coached a group of students in the art of polemics. He believed the best way to fully understand issues, required taking all positions into consideration prior to forming an opinion.

Dove was often requested to give lectures for benevolent organizations, and he never accepted a fee. He believed he had a responsibility to return to society a substantial portion of his earnings and talent. Dove also realized his lectures drew crowds that loved literature, and he felt fully compensated by their applause and the many novels they purchased.

Political Science was not Dove's calling, and he was reticent to flaunt his personal beliefs in his novels or their characters. His world views were moderate, believing that people should always be aware of the consequences of their actions. Government handouts without requirements were not something he approved, but he willingly provided financial and physical support to those who made an effort to improve their station. Dove claimed, "People or countries needing help must take positive steps to remove themselves from poverty and corruption."

Once Dove and Penny attended a lecture by a well known conservative that shocked the audience when he opened his remarks with, "After carefully examining my beliefs, I have determined that I am not conservative, but a true liberal." This made heads turn, and a groan rose from the attendees. He went on to say that many tasks he performs in life appear, on the surface, to be conservative, but on close evaluation are liberal. He said he had a wonderful dog that he loved dearly, so when the dog was put outside he tied the dog, restricting his freedom. That certainly sounded conservative, but he said he tied the dog to prevent the animal from running in the road and being killed by a car. Then he made the leap to children and being strict or permissive as parents. The speaker had a brother that pushed his freedom until he was on drugs, and currently his brother was in prison for being allowed his freedom at too early an age.

He talked about visiting his brother in prison, and he realized his brother had lost his liberty while the speaker was a liberal, free man. The argument resonated with Penny and Dove, particularly when he made examples of musicians and athletes that learn to follow the rules to develop their talent, rather than develop into an undisciplined musician or athlete that no one wants to see perform.

Dove often raised the law of unintended consequences when radical political decisions were offered from many quarters. Another favorite quote he used on this subject originated from Saint Bernard of Clairvau's proverb: "The road to hell is paved with good intentions." How often do people do something that seems to be the correct decision, only to have it backfire and turn into a terrible idea. Once Dove remarked, "I think of a woman who found a wallet containing several hundred dollars on the floor in a taxi, and promptly gave it to the cabbie, only to assure the wallet would never be returned to the rightful owner. That certainly is a good example, don't you think Penny?"

One of Dove's beliefs had to do with the unknowable subjects people dwell on in life. Religious themes like the Trinity Doctrine, Eucharist, life after death, and whether or not Jesus had a love affair with Mary Magdalene. The answers are unknowable, open for discussion but not suitable for serious argument. These are faith issues that people either believe or do not believe; but they cannot be proved. Dove believed the cause of homosexuality may be compared to the natural color of one's hair: uncontrollable. That is not to say there are not people who could have chosen to be straight who selected same sex partners. The new college aphorism is, "It is what it is." Dove held beliefs on all of these hot-button issues which often encumber society, but he never publicly discussed them because they were strictly opinions that in his judgment were unknowable.

Often these topics were explored in his novels with some of his most memorable characters being gay, bigots, political militants, right-to-lifers, priests, religious zealots, all with extreme positions. Dove presented these issues from both the positive and negative sides, allowing readers to render their individual decision.

Very clearly, Penny could recall Dove talking about many decades of relief the sad people of Haiti have required, and how the billions of dollars given to the country by Americans and others have not improved the people's lot in life. Being a preacher's kid, he had seen no improvement in Haiti since he was a small boy sixty years ago when their small church compassionately sent food and dollars to the starving. "It takes more than money to change a life or a country," he would privately say to Penny. "Disaster after disaster, and corrupt governments after corrupt governments have stifled the country, yet they continue in their same direction knowing the same expected results."

He would discuss neighboring countries to Haiti such as Jamaica, the Grand Cayman Islands and the Dominican Republic, not to mention Puerto Rico and the Virgin Islands that face the same weather strife year after year. He was perplexed with Haiti's inability to turn that poverty stricken, dictator controlled, beautiful country into a successful island as the others had many decades before. Dove wanted to see his endowments provide opportunities for long term positive change, not the continuation of the status quo.

Dove implemented the same principle when he provided extra help to students. He was quick to recognize and separate those interested in improving and those who were primarily interested in a better grade. Together as Penny and Dove became affluent from his success as an author, they shared their financial success, but they verified how charities used their money and how much their employees were compensated. They were interested in helping needy or decried people, not employing the rich and famous. Dove could understand the dichotomy between those who had already invested years or decades of labor to obtain financial security, and those that wanted an opportunity to succeed and raise their families outside poverty, but never invested in education or hard work. This was often the background material for his novels.

Dove and Penny were politically cut from the same mold. They were fiscally conservative but more liberal on social issues. They took the tact that few Americans are truly in favor of using abortion as a substitution for birth control, but they were never in favor of outlawing the procedure. Once in a debate they heard one team use the persuasive argument that abortion is pathetic unless it affects you or your family. They argued the hypothetical situation of the forty-five year old woman with two children in college who unexpectedly found she was pregnant. Following that, they went on to discuss the twelve year old expectant mother with the abusive father she and her mother were afraid to report to police. Once again, the law of unintended consequences comes in to play.

Though Dove was not involved in politics, he strongly believed sweeping democratic change was in order. He deplored the never-ending squabbles between the left and the right, and he believed neither political party had the wellbeing of the United States of America in mind as they created law. He always claimed he would write a novel about government one day.

Only after Dove reduced his teaching to one class per week did he start to slash travel for events. He often said he wanted to spend more time with Penny, gradually reducing his workload so they could fish together and enjoy each other's company. This also permitted more time for his novels, which had become, such a vital part of his life. Dove researched and wrote at least four hours daily, but occasionally he was in his office writing for ten or more hours before turning off the light and retiring for the day.

Some of Penny's most memorable experiences were those days fishing together. Dove had become such a tender person, he was a constant companion of joy. Often in some quiet place he would recite sonnets that came to mind from their surroundings, whether they were fishing or hiking an unfamiliar trail.

Other times he would reflect on a book he had completed or a movie he had seen recently, and often he raised the ethical issues or character flaws and delivered his thoughts on the work. Dove could have been a philosopher, an ethicist, a poet or a preacher had he chosen. One of the most surprising things about Dove was that he didn't look the part. Sometimes people think scholars should look like computer geeks, but Dove looked like an athlete. He had a powerful physique and the coordination that accompanied his brilliance right up until the moment he passed away on July 9, 2011, only 20 days after he and Penny celebrated their 46th anniversary of the day they met on that alluring mountain overlooking Peyto Lake. Over the years, that day became the one they cherished most of all.

On two occasions, Dove was selected to be a visiting professor, once at Oxford and a second time at Princeton. These opportunities presented unique occasions for them to explore, first England with all her history and theater, and then New York where they attended the theater a dozen times and visited the many historical locations on the East coast. They visited Stratford-upon-Avon where Dove brushed up on Shakespearean plays and the history of the Bard of Avon. When at Princeton, jumping on a train to Washington, Philadelphia or Boston for long weekends was exciting for both of them. Dove and Penny were thrilled to participate in big city life, but when they returned to their roots, they knew they were home, the place they loved most.

Dove and Penny were avid readers of newspapers and magazines, more than watchers of TV news. They never ceased to be amazed at how poor judgment is responsible for incredible sadness and regrets. Many times when they read a story about an unhinged person or group of people they would say, "Now here's something that defines the word, 'unreasonableness.'" It became a game to identify these articles first and shout out, "Unreasonableness."

They noticed a lack of common sense affects all types of people regardless of their color, religion, sex, wealth, education or position in life. Poor judgment is displayed in what politicians say, poor judgment implemented by police officers who lose their tempers, poor judgment when carrying a weapon without authorization, poor judgment when posting remarks or photos on the internet, and most importantly, poor judgment when leaving children alone in a car. There is no end to the people in this world who are sitting in jail because they couldn't control their tempers in a civil manner.

There are always excuses for unreasonable behavior. The schoolteacher was in love with his or her student and couldn't control his or her feelings. The policeman just lost control when he beat a man to death because he was speeding. The mother drowned her children because her boyfriend would not marry her until the babies were out of her life. There is always some excuse that is incomprehensible to most people. With twenty-four hour news programming, these tragedies have turned into entertainment, and the public gets to hear attorneys generate excuses that justify the actions.

Sometimes Dove and Penny talked about justice in the old wild west being more fair and reasonable than the current system of incarcerating people for decades while their case is tried, reviewed, appealed and then often dismissed on some creative technicality. Taxpayers pay huge sums to prosecute guilty people, only to have cases acquitted or overthrown. It's not always about guilt or innocence, too often it is the quality of lawyers and the quantity of dollars provided by the defendant.

Penny and Dove once knew a young man who had a catholic priest for a professor. The student was arrested for running a traffic light. He mentioned it to the priest, and the priest said, "I'll take care of it for you." The priest negotiated a plea bargain which reduced the charge to having a noisy muffler, which resulted in a smaller fine and no points on his driving record. Now is that justice?

The day passed quickly as Penny reminisced about their thoughts and conversations, and when she looked at her watch she realized she had been in the chapel for three hours. At times, she listened to a student play an instrument or a quartet sing, but mostly Penny quietly remembered Dovie and how their minds were on the same page as they explored and lived life together.

Penny wished Dove was here this year to see his Wolverines atop the league standings, but most of all, she wished he was here to hold her hand and whisper that he loved her as he held her close, comforted her, and dried her fresh tears. Dove was a true Wolverine fan with a college spirit seldom seen! Perhaps he had a bird's eye view from the heavens.

Chapter 49
Remembering Penny's Career

Penny's life as a school teacher, especially the years she taught high school were mixed with love for students and disappointment in the school system. Discipline was never a problem in her classes because with every new class she lay the groundwork as to her expectations. With every first class each year, she and her students came to an agreement about expectations they should have of her, and she of them. More than any other day, she followed a script to be sure everything was covered, and she took notes as the students gave their expectations after careful prodding. The following day they all signed a pledge agreeing to grades, behavior, homework, tests and attendance. Once the rules were developed and agreed, discipline was easy.

Students knew what she required, and she knew what they expected. Penny was always respectful to her students, and the courtesy was returned. Another day during the first few weeks was designed to prepare students for life after high school. They talked about requirements to gain entrance to college, and they discussed why it is imperative to prepare for the future. Penny liked to tell them about the smart boy who completed only the minimum requirements to graduate, and then was unable to get into a premed program because he didn't learn higher math, chemistry or Latin. All of those courses are required to enter a program to study medicine.

"Think about what you want to do with your life," Penny used to preach, "soon nearly every employee will need a high school diploma to earn a decent wage to support a family. Are you planning to get married and have children someday? Do you want to live in a nice home, have enough groceries to feed your children, and do you want to have a dependable car? If you have no expectations, you will never be disappointed; but if you hope to be happy and provide happiness to others, please do your very best in this class, and every other class."

"You may not realize it now, but auto mechanics require talented people who can troubleshoot using the process of elimination. Carpenters, electricians and plumbers need math skills to know their costs, and determine the price of a project. Everyone clearly needs to speak and write the King's English properly to be successful in life. People need to be able to understand you before they will hire you. Last but not least, you must be a nice person others want to work with and trust. If you aren't trustworthy, life can be difficult with your spouse, your employers and the police. Now I am only talking about life's basic requirements to live with joy, pride and love."

Many students, over the years, came back later, or sent Penny letters to tell her how much those two hours in her class helped them grow-up and take responsibility for their lives. Thankfully, she still remembers many of their names and loves them to this day. Penny had a fabulous career as a school teacher, even though many may think her success was secondary to Dove's. Penny would not trade her years with high school students for Dove's career writing and teaching college, as she knew both were extremely important.

Chapter 50
Penny's Public School Thoughts

Dove and Penny both had considerable concerns with the public schools in America, and the perceived importance of gaining a quality education. Voters feel they pay exorbitant sums of money to hire teachers, build facilities and provide transportation to offer opportunities for every American student. Still, when the ink dries on the diplomas, too few students are appropriately prepared to earn an income commensurate with their expectations, or maintain the lifestyle their parents provided them in their first eighteen years of life.

Teachers have completed college degree programs in at least one specialized field such as mathematics, science, social sciences or English, along with learning how to teach their subject. Many teachers complain about class size and student behavior being difficult to control, and they know students desiring to excel are hindered by the diverse classroom distractions and disruptive classmates. In many school systems, students enter school speaking no English whatsoever, and the cost of educating them overwhelms the taxpayer. Although most teachers agree that many coworkers are failures, their unions have become ossified and often protect members and make it nearly impossible to terminate these underachievers and hire motivated replacements.

Parents are the voters, and they are the ones paying the bills. They have seen their real estate taxes soar to the point many pay more for taxes than for their mortgage. When little Johnny and Mary begin kindergarden the parents are active in their progress and are involved in their learning, but by the time the child reaches fifth or sixth grade their interest wanes, and they rarely darken the school halls until serious issues arise or for a sports event. They wash their hands and blame teachers for their child's failure.

Having been career teachers, Dove and Penny knew there was blame enough for all parties involved, but solutions have been few and far between. The differences between being a high school teacher and a college professor are vast and many, because the onus is transferred to the student from the parent and the educator in college.

Parents pay tens of thousands of dollars to provide a college education for each child, usually that much in a single year, and they are reticent to spend good money after bad. When Penny attended her first class lecture, the Academic Dean had everyone stand and look at the person on either side of them, and then he said, "One of the two students on either side of you will not graduate from here. Many will drop out during the first semester, and many more after the end of the first year. The decision is yours. We provide quality teachers, but you need to be a quality learner if you plan to graduate from Penn State."

He continued, "The difference, you see, is in responsibility. In high school, teachers and your parents were responsible to see you graduate, but in college, the responsibility lies with you. Some of you will find you are not mature enough to accept the challenge. Some of you will not have the desire to focus on a long-term objective that will determine how you live your life, and how satisfied you will be as you mature to adulthood. College is an endeavor to obtain the building blocks to be a successful, contributing member of society who leads their country to achieve higher living standards for all Americans and even the entire world."

The Academic Dean continued, "Some of you may not like every required course you are enrolled, but this great university requires every student to successfully complete each one before they can graduate. There are very few exceptions. You do, or you do not meet the prerequisites required. Summing up this message, I want you to know that we want you to succeed and become a graduate of Penn State. We want you to make a difference, whether you choose to become a teacher, a lawyer, a doctor, a chemist, an engineer, a historian, a linguist, an author or a business professional. The choice is yours! If you do your part, the university will provide you with the essential tools for success. Now, let's be sure you are not one of the many who drop out because you are too tired to attend classes or too busy to meet the professor's expectations. The choice is yours."

That first lecture impressed Penny considerably. She looked carefully at the students on either side and wanted to be sure she was not one who withdrew from college, for any reason! Inside, she was grateful that her professors would not permit wisecrackers to disrupt classes, and it was that first lecture that persuaded her to enter the field of education. Penny wanted to teach school, and provide a positive direction for youngsters as they navigated their adolescent years.

Chapter 51
Dove's Memorial Service

The day was September 21, the first day of fall, and the day of Dove's Memorial and Celebration of his life. The chapel was filled to capacity that day, as Dove's memorial service was open to the entire student body at Grove City College. As Penny was escorted to the front row by Dr. Smith, President of the College, she could hear Bach's *Air on a G String* being performed by six college seniors on stringed instruments.

The glorious music played at least thirty minutes as the seats filled. Her nieces and nephews along with their children and grandchildren were all seated together. One by one Penny wept for her brothers, her parents, Dove's parents and now her late husband of forty-six years, Doctor Jon Scott. Dove was the only love of her life, and the pain and emptiness from his absence was horrendous and never-ending. Unwittingly, sometimes she still turns to ask him a question, and then she catches herself talking to an empty room.

Nights are particularly lonely when she lies in bed, lonesome for his familiar touch and soft, kind voice whispering in the dark. He is not there to kiss her good-night or grip her hand before falling off in slumber. It is then when she cries for him and knows he can never comfort her again. She survives the days because she keeps busy with the same commitments they had together, but when nightfall comes Penny's heart cannot be consoled. Oh, for just one more day with Dove!

The new chapel pastor, Dr. Charles Morris, came to the microphone and offered a prayer followed by a reading of Psalm 23, Dove's favorite Bible passage. A soprano began *Pie Jesu*, accompanied by Dr. Andrew Voss, Chairman of Grove City Music Department on the old manual four Kimball Organ along with three female violinists, all seniors. Dove would love to have heard the inspiring music presented for him, including his favorite Bach piece, *Air*.

The eulogy was offered by Dr. Smith followed by several faculty members reminiscing about Dove's skill as a teacher, friend, leader, counselor, author and husband. Four students spoke, remembering how Dove had influenced them in their studies, but more importantly they reflected that they were better people for having known and studied under Dr. Scott. She wept again for her love, and she wept for the kind words spoken on his behalf. Penny wanted to speak, but she knew she would be unable to maintain her composure and, therefore, declined.

The Executive Director for the Stevens Home for Unwed Mothers, Mrs. Jean Carol RN, spoke of the endowment that was bequeathed to maintain and fund their operations in both Warren and Grove City. She told of how her life was changed because of the Stevens Home, and how she was planning suicide before she was rescued from the unforgiving society she had been raised. Then she told how loving others, like herself, and helping them recover from critical personal failure is her life's ambition.

The final speaker was the Reverend Bobby Morris, who mentioned his near fatal injury playing football and pointed towards Thorn Field. He told of Dove's companionship and how every weekend his lifelong best friend stayed at his bedside for hours, inspiring him to endure the pain and live a full life helping others more unfortunate than himself. His prodding and support was a key factor in his survival, and then he said, "God makes people in all shapes, colors, intellects and with different hearts. I have never known a person to have more compassion and love than Dr. Jon Scott, and I ask God to be generous with this giant of a man who has changed the world with his incredible novels. Penny's and Dove's generosity to his fellow men and women has made a difference. They gave until it hurt." The tall, thin African American former Grove City College quarterback returned to his seat with a slight limp and tears in his eyes.

The service ended with *Panis Angelicus* as attendees filed out after the closing benediction. Penny knew Dove's students loved him, but she did not know that nearly every student for thirty years sat in one of his composition classes. The outpouring of love from his students along with the many references to his novels was something Penny shall never forget. Dove's memorial service was perfect. His parents would have been proud of their son and his many accomplishments, but most of all they would be proud of the way he lived his life, the happiness he brought others, and the constant state of joy he brought to his wife of forty-six years.

Chapter 52
Remembering Trudy's Gift

Today as she thinks back on Trudy with her difficult younger years, Penny bubbles over with pride. Tru and Brian have two boys and two girls who are the pride and joy of grandma. Dove loved to take the grandchildren to their little cottage, deep in the woods, and teach them to fish and hike the trails, just like he taught Tru. They learned to identify nearly every tree in the forest, by the shape and color of their leaves, the seeds, and its form or structure. He taught them to respect nature and all of God's freely given gifts. The little ones are now all in their twenties, and Penny is a great-grandma with three beautiful boys. Soon two more will be sitting on her lap as she swings on the front porch and sings them sweet lullabies. They all live within an easy drive of Warren and Grove City, so they will always be close.

When Penny lost Dovie, Trudy and Brian and usually one or two of her grandchildren visited Penny at least once every week. They drove down to Grove City from Titusville every Saturday to comfort her, and usually take her out for dinner.

Trudy was the second most glorious gift in Penny's life, far exceeding her highest hopes. She has truly been the gift that keeps on giving, the child she never planned, but the child who makes her life complete.

Dovie loved his daughter. He loved the way she smiled, he adored her inquisitiveness, and he loved her warm, sensitive and compassionate nature. The one thing Dovie worried about when Trudy came to live with them, was if she could ever love a man after her violent rape at the hands of Frank Johnson. Dove confided that he agonized Trudy would never be close to him, and never fully trust him; but those were wasted concerns. Tru, as he loved to call her, warmed to Dovie, almost as fast as Penny during that fateful June in the Canadian Rockies, and soon she could peer out a window and see them hand in hand walking through the meadow together, father and daughter.

Penny wishes she had taken more photos of them when they were walking or fishing together, or when they were just searching for a new adventure. Penny imagines everyone has those regrets after their child is grown. Trudy was a gift, one that brightened their lives and helped them enjoy life's mysteries together. Trudy is the gift that keeps on giving, and Dove was the consummate father Tru needed, and he was the perfect husband and lover for Penny!

Chapter 53
Great Expectations

Dove genuinely attempted to make every novel more exciting, more insightful and replete with examples of successful people striving to meet attainable objectives. He also created people who lived from day-to-day without any thought where they were heading in life. Of great concern to Dove and Penny, were millions of people that didn't know the magnificent American lives others lived. They too often lived in poverty with no assets, with only food stamps and a welfare check.

The problem seems to be unconquerable. There is a point which one passes that is truly the point of no return. They never were taught to prepare for their future, and once they dropped out of school, it was almost always too late for them to overcome their disadvantage.

On the other hand, as life passed them by, they could see the success of others who had prepared for life, and spent years training for a successful career. It was when the uneducated recognized their shortcomings that they too wanted success;

and unfortunately, they were totally unequipped for the life they saw others living.

People who have diligently worked towards success often have empathy for those who are unsuccessful in life, and many are willing to help in the form of giving more and better government benefits to them. Too few, however, are willing to stand up to the plate and dig in their own pocket to support the needy and uneducated.

This is where the political paradox occurs. Citizens are torn as they try to resolve the issue of the haves and the have nots. One group wants to take from the rich and redistribute their wealth to the poor through higher taxes, while the other faction wants the poor to earn their way out of poverty as many of the wealthy have accomplished through education and hard work. While the government struggles with the incredible costs of education, increasingly more and more teachers are needed to teach in Spanish and special education. The main-stream children are the disadvantaged because their education suffers as more and more money is spent on individual programs which do not help the main-streamed youth gain the knowledge they need to be successful in life.

Dove had a fascinating facility to present his views as he built his characters, but as brilliant as he was, he always came back to H. L. Mencken's quote, "For every complex problem there is an answer that is clear, simple, and wrong." Penny believed Dove had the compassion to love and support those who were unable to live life as they would have hoped, but he also believed throwing more money at the problem will never modify the results. Save winning the lottery, only education and hard work can bring people from poverty to wealth.

Once Dove came home from the college library with a large stack of copies. He said, "Penny, I've been searching through some resources which offer surprises for me. Many of today's politicians and extremely wealthy Americans pay little in taxes because they shelter their riches with complex trusts, only they can afford. Yet they are the powers who want other Americans to pay more to support their beliefs." That's when he said, "I can feel another novel coming on." Unfortunately, that book was never written, but Penny knows a file exists with many of his ideas.

Chapter 54
Jameela

Six months have passed since Dovie passed away. Penny loves to think about Dove, but theirs wasn't the only true love in their family. Penny thinks of her parents and the deep love they nurtured through decades of hard work and often trying times. She also thinks of her brother, Ron, and his wife, Jenna, who had a crucial family issue to resolve and how love helped them make the right decision.

Their son, Craig, met a girl when they were in medical school at Johns Hopkins University who could have caused a big family stir. Craig was close friends with Amon Hassan, a fraternity brother from undergraduate school, when he was introduced to Jameela, Amon's twin sister. She had just graduated from Brown University and returned home to live with her brother and father as was customary for Muslims until they marry. She was just beginning medical school, and as it turned out, Craig was in the same program, but they had not met until Amon made the introduction. Craig fell in love with this knockout beautiful Kuwaiti girl of the Islamic faith.

Fearing the repercussions from both sets of parents, Craig and Jameela fell in love after knowing one another for less than four months. They planned to elope to marry, but at the last moment, Craig decided his parents deserved to know about his fiancé. Craig called home and broke the news of the woman in his life, and was caught completely by surprise when his father said, "Mom and I will be out on Saturday to meet Jameela." Then Ron went on to say that he and Jenna had gone to the library before they visited Craig and Jameela to learn more about her customs and faith. They learned that Jameela means beautiful, graceful and lovely in Arabic, and they were not disappointed.

Penny remembers asking Ron about the situation and he said, "Jenna and I talked about this for every waking moment, from the time Craig called until the time we met his beautiful fiancé at dinner that first evening. Perhaps it would have been easy to reject her before we met, but it was apparent they loved each other fervently. She was so beautiful with her sparkling dark eyes and long, straight, shiny black hair that nearly reached her tiny waist, I could see why he was attracted to her. When Jameela opened her mouth and began to speak, she spoke perfect American English. Her soft, suntanned skin was slightly darker than Craig's, and after warm hugs and a few tears, we accepted her at once. She was truly gorgeous! We knew it was either accept a new daughter-in-law or lose our only son, and the decision was easy."

Ron and Jenna asked Jameela if she had talked with her father and brother about her plans to wed their son, and she responded that she was afraid to consider asking for permission. Although her brother knew of their plans, she had not revealed their love or intentions to her father. Jameela began to cry, and she admitted that sometimes Muslims renounce daughters when they are disobedient and reject their parent's wishes. Jameela knew her father loved her and would never harm her physically, but she dreaded rejection from someone she loved deeply. She knew her father loved her immensely and was always kind and loving towards her, but she also knew her father would never agree to the marriage. Craig suggested Jameela should stay at their house until the wedding and call her father to ask for his blessing. The evening before the marriage, Jameela called her father to explain her love for Craig and that she wanted him to attend the event. When she returned from making the call, Jamella reported she was disowned by her family, and she was in tears. Her father threatened her with pledges to never see or talk to her again and slammed the phone into its cradle. His loss was the Stevens family's gain!

As the years passed, Jameela was a constant companion to her mother-in-law; and she cared for Jenna in her final days. When Dovie passed away, Jameela flew to be at Penny's side to help her though that first lonely week when she was alone and most despondent. Penny learned Jameela had the compassion and understanding that consoled her and helped her navigate the unchartered depths of losing her lifelong partner and lover. Jameela continues to call Penny every Saturday to check how she's doing, and two times since Penny lost Dovie, she has flown out to share her weekend in Grove City. Penny always loved Jameela, from the first time she met her at the civil wedding. Penny loved her spontaneous and committed love affair with Craig, and how she shares her love so openly and freely. Penny loves how she has adopted Christmas as her most celebrated holiday with decorations inside and outside her lovely home, and she loves how she honors her God and Penny's God.

Chapter 55
Penny's Last Visit to the Chapel

Penny continues to pine for Dovie just like others yearn for their lover when they are taken away. Her anguish is deep and painful, but it may not be any greater than others experience when their cheerful life is filled with the pain from their longing. She came to the chapel again knowing this will be her last visit. The brief chapel service was completed, and the students were all parading toward the exit and heading to their next class.

For many weeks, Penny has thought about their splendid, epic love story while sitting in this very pew, listening to the talented speakers and inspirational music. She has made the decision that will take her away from Grove City and the college she loves, to retake control of her life. Penny has work to complete before she leaves this world for the next, and the sooner she begins, the sooner she will put her grief aside.

She recognizes that her family is gone. They have pretty much passed away, and there is no one remaining to go back to, or on whom to lean. Her parents are gone, her loving brothers are gone, but their adult children carry on the family traditions. They are excellent examples of people who understand America and for what she stands. They live every day of their lives supporting their conscience.

Of my grand nieces and nephews, the closest are Craig and Jameela Stevens' beautiful daughters. Penny continues to mourn Jameela's loss of her father. He couldn't come to grips with Jameela breaking with tradition, and marrying without his blessing outside his faith. He disowned her and never spoke to her again until just before his death. While he was being treated for terminal cancer, he finally called and forgave her. Bless Jameela for forgiving and traveling to the Middle East on three occasions to comfort him and be with him during his time of need. Nevertheless, he could never retrieve those decades without his daughter and his beautiful granddaughters.

While Penny's here, she is recognized as the wife of a distinguished novelist and an exceptional professor, but she is not recognized for who she is in Grove City. Penny plans to go back to Warren and buy a small home on East Street in the downtown area where she can walk wherever she chooses. Penny knows the town has changed since her childhood. Many of the beautiful homes have become dilapidated over the years and are in a severe state of disrepair. Some haven't been painted or re-roofed for decades, and many of the wrap-around porches have been taken down because of the cost of repair and the scarcity of good-paying jobs nowadays.

There are many people still alive who will know Penny from her school days, teaching years, or perhaps from the wonderful Stevens Home. There's also Jean Carroll, the young lady who became so influential in her life after being one of the first residents there. Jean helped Penny with her recovery after losing her baby. Of all the women who passed through the Stevens Home, Jean was the most successful of all. Not only did she earn her GED, she became a Registered Nurse. Additionally Penny will spend some of her summer days at the rustic cottage in Heart's Content when her grandchildren visit. That's an outstanding place to relax with a book or just wet a line.

Jean's success and continued involvement in the Stevens Home charity has been a true inspiration in Penny's life. Too often people accept help and never return the favor, but not Jean. She is now the Executive Director of the Stevens Home, and Penny plans to assist her in every way she can. Another stalwart supporter of these troubled women is Jill Harrison Powers. The former terrified teen who confided her pregnancy to Penny so many years earlier, continues her work with unwed mothers. Her mother and father also contributed untold time to make Penny's dream the success it is today.

Perhaps, with all the penning of Dove's career and success, Penny may leave the impression she had a boring or less meaningful life, but the contrary was true. Teaching high school students was a privilege for her, for she was a role model and provided understanding and counseling, as students struggled with adolescence. These were the children she never had as her own, but they made her proud that she could know them and help shape their lives.

She hates to leave today, knowing that this was where Dove was happiest; nevertheless, while she is in Warren, Penny will be just a few blocks away from where his body now rests. Penny will be able to walk up the little hill that overlooks the peaceful river and rest on his tombstone. Soon, her body will join him there, but her spirit will meet with his when they reach out for each other on that beautiful shore. Can't you hear the music?

In the sweet by and by,
We shall meet on that beautiful shore;

In the sweet by and by,
We shall meet on that beautiful shore.
Lyrics: Sanford Bennett, 1868
Composer Joseph Webster

Chapter 56
Penny Learns the Secret

Today is a dark and snowy day as Penny sits in Grove City College's Harbison Chapel. What light there is from outside barely penetrates the stained glass, and only darker shadows dim the nave before her. She must remember Christmas is approaching rapidly, and snow is typical for Western Pennsylvania. Penny heard on the radio there are only three shopping days remaining, but her gifts are purchased and wrapped. She expects Christmas will be lonesome without her Dovie to hold her and surprise her with some exciting gift. Nevertheless, Penny looks forward to spending the holidays with Trudy, Brian and their children, grandchildren and their extended families. Penny promises she will have a glorious Christmas, though an aching void lingers in her fractured heart. Again the music stretches towards the heavens as Penny once again thinks about Dove. She didn't plan to return here today, or ever again, when she departed three weeks ago, but there has been a critical revelation since then. Therefore, she returned to meditate about something she just learned December 3 that shocked her to the soul like a thunderbolt from above. Today, Penny is wondering if she needs to ask forgiveness, as she dwells on this mortifying news. She had never been so humiliated, and Penny was unsure how best to handle the situation.

Penny has been sorting through Dove's many files since she was last here in the chapel. There are files for characters, story plots, beginnings of novels, and notes for the classes he taught at Grove City College. Additionally, there was one file named, "Scanned Data." Dove and Penny have Macintosh computers, mainly because Apple is so popular among educators, and she thought they were so much easier to use. Dove used his iMac more than Penny, because of his prolific writing, but one day last week while she looked through his computer, she opened the "Scanned Data" folder, and inside was another file he named *The Secret Never Shared*. First, when she noticed the document, Penny assumed it contained notes for another novel or short story, for he had three or four manuscripts underway at all times. This was particularly true since he became Professor Emeritus of Literature and Creative Writing, and taught only one course each semester and none during the summer.

Actually, as Penny started to investigate the files, she observed the novels were in various stages of development. *The Secret Never Shared* file, however, contained over one hundred pages of handwritten notes and some fifty photocopies which he had scanned and inserted into the computer file. One could see these informational pages were placed in the file, piecemeal. The recorded dates indicated only one or two entries were created on any day, and the dates extended over numerous years. One of the files contained his latest manuscript titled, *The Secret Never Shared*, with a final entry date only three days before he passed away. Clearly the novel was well underway, with over two hundred pages of manuscript divided into different chapters. The turbid facts were all there, but the novel was obviously incomplete. The concluding chapter was missing, and he had still not disclosed the secret in the novel.

Every manuscript on Dove's computer had a corresponding paper file filled with copious notes; however, *The Secret Never Shared* file, had no paper records or notes whatsoever, leading Penny to question his new procedure of writing. Or had Dove been frightened she might stumble upon a written file? At first when she saw the computer file Penny thought, "Wow, that's a captivating title." Each time she saw the novel title it intrigued her further, until two weeks ago when she eventually read through the scans and notes. There were documents from the Franklin Library, copies of birth certificates, newspaper articles and handwritten notes containing meaningful information on both Dove and her. Penny could barely comprehend the secret he had kept for so long. As she thought about her discovery, she was reminded of the law of unintended consequences, for first Dove, and now Penny, never intended to learn this dismal secret that troubled, first his life, and now hers.

Quite clearly, Dove believed he and Penny were full brother and sister, and he had lived with this stressful knowledge for twenty years. For nearly one-half of their married lives, Dove knew they were siblings, yet he never shared his private knowledge with Penny, the one he loved and trusted with everything, even his life. Dove had collected vast quantities of information, but on further inspection, he never researched his mother's side of the family and that surprised Penny immensely.

How could this be? There were no clues, no gossipy relatives or neighbors. Dove was just an intellectually curious man pondering his past, searching to acquire facts. He needed to know, who he was, and from whom and where he came. Her first reaction that morning was that these were details for another novel, then as reality set in, disbelief penetrated Penny's mind. After the immediate denial, her anger lashed out at Dove, then the shock settled in and pierced her heart. Her anger quickly changed to disappointment and sadness instead of anger. Then Penny's mourning commenced.

Why would Dove keep such a monumental enigma to himself, instead of sharing with his lover of forty-six years? Oh, Penny could understand a slight delay while he reflected on his new knowledge, but never broaching the subject for more than twenty years? That didn't sound like her Dovie. They had no secrets from one another, certainly nothing consequential like this. She knew all the works that he was writing, or at least Penny thought she knew each one. Often he asked her opinion on a plot or a character in a novel, and occasionally he asked her to read a chapter aloud, so he could hear the cadence of the words. How could he do this to her? Perhaps she needs to dwell on this issue herself and consider the possible reason he never confided with her.

Is it possible Dovie tried to share his secret with Penny? Did she miss the subtle signals he sent? Did he try to broach this humiliating subject when Penny wasn't listening? Was she to blame for his silence? Penny needed to think long and hard about this entire situation that developed over the last two decades, and of Dove hiding a hugely important secret from her. Then, she needed to consider what reaction she would have had, if she had been the one to learn the secret, and he had no knowledge! Could Penny have chanced losing Dovie by telling him that they were siblings? Could that have been why he concealed the secret?

Now she has had a chance to dig a little deeper into Dove's and her genealogy over the past two weeks, Penny learned considerably more information about her Grandmother

Swanson. She grasped more than she ever wanted to know! Dove did not include notes about their grandmother or grandfather Swanson. Penny still finds it incredulous that he never pursued the Swanson's genealogy! Is it plausible he knew mother's ancestors and had that data in a different location on the computer? How could he not know? Would it be Dove was unable to accept the way their mother was treated in her time of need, and he refused to turn over those stones?

This week, Penny learned that Maggie Davidson was their mother. Maggie's mother was Perle Columbe Swanson, daughter of Pierre and Marie Columbe from Pittsburgh. Perle and Abel Swanson moved to Warren where they were married in 1915, only five months before she delivered her first son, Jean Paul. When Penny pieced everything together, she recalled the adage, "an apple never falls far from the tree," and she wondered if that is unquestionably true. Could it be that Perle was punishing her daughter for the same mistake she had made twenty-five years earlier? Penny contemplated the complexity of the issue, and she was deeply concerned that forgiveness didn't seem to be in the equation.

Then her instincts kicked into gear, and she realized Columbe was the French word for Dove, and she understood why Maggie called her son "Dovie." Penny's research affirms Dove and she are Pierre and Marie Columbe's great-grandchildren. Dovie had to know this, because he was fluent in French! He must have known, but there were no files.

At first, when Penny learned Dove and her were siblings, and already knowing that his mother called him Dovie, she thought maybe she could trace their forefathers back to Otto Dove, whose name was elegantly engraved in the stone quarry, so many years before. She's not sure why, but at first, Penny was disappointed when she learned they were from the Columbe family, for she imagined Dovie coming from the Doves, the proud stone quarry people from Warren.

Penny studied French too, but she wasn't fluent like Dove; nevertheless, Penny knew Columbe was the French word for Dove, thus the nickname, Dovie. It was clear there is much more work to complete before she can publish Dove's final novel, but of this Penny is sure: they are brother and sister from the Columbe and Swanson families, originally from Pittsburgh, PA, and the Davidson *and* Miller Families from Franklin, PA. Dove had researched the Millers, and Davidsons thoroughly but she expects many months will pass before the Swanson's and Columbe's genealogy work is complete.

Though today, Penny is upset with Dovie for hiding this incredible secret from her, she has already forgiven, and she will continue to love and adore her Dovie forever and ever. Yes, she's hurt and disappointed he couldn't bring himself to trust her love and commitment, and share the secret with her, but Penny could never push Dovie away or out of her life. She could only love him. She can't help her feelings for him. You see, Penny believes God works in ways she does not always understand, and she believes their meeting at the Peyto Lake overview took some planning, and some weighty coordinating, and it wasn't Dovie or she who set the agenda.

As she stands to leave the chapel, darkness is approaching and Penny can see Christmas lights and symbols decorating the beautiful campus. Taking one final tear glazed view towards the nave and the beautiful sanctuary, it occurs to her that she has lived many more days than she has days ahead, but her remaining days will be used to complete Dove's last novel, *The Secret Never Shared*. The question in Penny's mind is, "Should she share her new found knowledge with Trudy and her family, or should she continue the charade and have the book published upon her death?"

When this book is published, Penny's and Dove's heritage will be as clear as a fresh water trout stream in the Canadian Rockies. Today, this genealogy information is simply too murky and complicated to consider. Perhaps she needs to be like Scarlet O'Hara in *Gone With the Wind*, when she was lonely for Tara, lonely for the Old South, and lonely for the life she lost saying, "Home, I'll go home ... After all, Tomorrow is another day!"

The End

Epilogue

Here, I am Dovie! What a beautiful afternoon as I sit beside your newly erected tombstone. I am confident that you would approve my selection, modest though it is. Remember our journey to Ireland when you were preparing to teach a new course in Irish literature? I never forgot that trip, particularly the engraved cemetery marker written by an unknown poet that recorded: "Death leaves a heartache no one can heal, love leaves a memory no one can steal." Those words reflect my love and my loss for the most incredible husband a woman could ever have. I had that meaningful poem etched beneath your name, to remind future generations of our love and my loss.

The pristine Allegheny River gently flows today, though we had a torrential rainfall and the forest remains deep with winter's snowy blanket. The massive Kinzua Dam rigidly controls spring's flooding rage by stifling the relentless river flow in northwestern Pennsylvania. This Army Corp of Engineers' retention project permits rivers and creeks to evacuate the melting spring snow and rains into the lower Allegheny River basin peaceably. Our serene love story migrated through many chapters like this gentle river that winds through small, sleepy towns, large cities, narrow rapids and peaceful forests, from its source to the deep blue sea.

Today is Mother's Day, and like we always did together, I went to church this morning with our family. Trudy and Brian came early this morning and brought Susie and Jenny, their newest twin granddaughters. That makes five great-grandchildren now Dovie. They're so cute you would just love them; and their big brothers are so proud of their baby sisters. Who would ever have believed we would have great-grandchildren?

Last night I dreamed about you Dovie. My dream was so vivid I can recall the clothes you wore, the words you spoke, and exactly where we were. Often I dream of you, but never before have I had such an evocative dream. You held my hand again, and wrapped your long, slender fingers around mine, just like when we walked together along a winding, silent path, busy with God's gifts of Christmas ferns, rhododendrons, trillium and lady slippers.

Like today, the weather was beautiful, warm temperatures with clear blue skies and small puffy clouds; and I had a view down a mountainside where an azure blue lake, shaped like a horse's head, lay in the valley below. Birds were singing, and new candles of fragrant growth were forming on the tall green fir trees. Behind us, a lone elk grazed on a higher bluff in the meadow. Spring is such an optimistic time of the year I feel as a yoke has been lifted from me.

Dove, you talked to me in my dream! This is the first dream where you talked to me, and your voice was clear and deep, just like always. You were wearing my favorite shirt, the blue denim shirt with the western snaps in place of buttons. Remember the faded shirt with the frayed collar from being washed so many times? You looked the same as the day you left me, still the handsome man I loved from the first day we met.

Now, I want to affirm one more time I love you, Dovie. You provided for my happiness for forty-six years. Thanks to you, we adopted a teenage girl who gave us love in return, along with our grandchildren and great-grandchildren. I confess I wasn't sure I wanted to rescue Trudy because I still held out hope we would have our own children. Adopting Trudy was the singularly best thing we ever did, Dovie. Thank you for having a better vision of the future than I.

Last night you said you still love me, too. I thank you for that. You also were so apologetic for the secret you never shared, the one you had kept for so many years. I hope I can put your mind at ease, when I say you protected me all of those years. You saved me from knowing and worrying, about something I had no knowledge and no control. Perhaps, you were worried I would have left you once I learned the secret, but Dove, nothing could ever separate you from me, other than death.

I hope you visit me often in my dreams, Dovie. I want you to relive with me the happy life we spent together. Also, I want to read the novel I am completing for you, *The Secret Never Shared.* I want you to point out how I can make it better, and use some of the beautiful words and phrases only you possess.

Oh, by the way, I have met some of our Columbe relatives right here in Warren. Most have moved away over the years, but I have met two families who live in Warren, and I understand there are more within twenty-five miles. This summer I plan to have a reunion to learn more of our ancestors we have never met. I have traced some of our heritage back to our great-grandparents, but I have yet to delve into the Swansons and Johnsons.

The Warren Public Library has an extensive genealogy section with old census data, newspapers and books that helped trace our history, Dovie. I even found a book reporting we have ancestors who were wounded in the Civil War. I'll tell you all about our relatives when we meet again. I'm also working on the stone quarry story you were interested in writing. I'm researching about how the huge stones were removed from the side hill, and transported to downtown Warren. I have distressing news on that though. The beautiful engraved stone is there no more. An oil wellhead is at the base of the stone quarry, and all of the large rocks are either gone or destroyed.

Trudy and Brian are taking me out to dinner with their little granddaughters for Mother's Day Dinner. We're going to Chiodo's Ferro Cucina, a small restaurant at the West End. I don't think it was here when we lived in Warren, but as you know, nothing stays the same. Dove, I hope you visit me in another dream real soon. We can talk about our wedding, our little cottage in the forest or maybe Buddy. Speaking of Buddy, I have started to shop around for a little Sheltie to keep me company, so the next time I visit, I may bring a friend.

I have come full circle in my life, Dovie. I have returned to Warren, the town where I was raised. I never admitted this before, even to myself, but as I think back, I was lonely in my high school years. I was lonely for the companionship of a young man. During college, I wanted to find Mr. Right, but he was too illusive, and part of my life was empty. You were God's answer to my many prayers, some nearly desperate, as I looked for the man I wanted to spend life loving. Until you and I awkwardly met I searched but never came close to finding my dream. Thanks to you, Dovie, I was never lonely for those forty-six years when you were with me. Since you've been gone, my heart feels the same lonely emptiness as before we met. I continue to long for you. You are my life's light that has dimmed, and flickers not, but my love for you will never die.

Perhaps the next time I come, Dovie, you would like me to play some of your favorite classical music on your iPOD. I'll be waiting to see you in a dream again soon, and, please never give another thought to keeping the secret from me. I am proud of you. Everyplace we ever went together, I was incredibly proud of the brilliant and handsome man who always held my hand. I'm proud that you loved me, and tried to spare me the hurt, pain and suffering I may have endured; and I'm proud of my brother and my faithful husband who cared for me until the very end. I love you Dovie; I'll always love you!

218

About the Author

James H. Dove

Mr. Dove graduated from Warren High School in 1959 before joining the US Navy. Jim served during the Cold War from 1959 to 1963 aboard the USS Triton, one of the world's first and largest nuclear powered submarines. He graduated from Roberts Wesleyan College in Rochester, NY in 1967 with a BA in English.

After twenty years in various sales and marketing positions with Eastman Kodak in several U.S. Cities, he returned to Rochester, NY where he managed Federal Government sales and instrumentation products worldwide, until he retired from Kodak in 1992. Jim was VP, General Manager and on the Board of Directors of Intellisoft CPI for nine years prior to fully retiring in 2001.

Mr. Dove is a former Chairman of the Board of Trustees of the First Congregational Church of East Bloomfield, NY and is an Ordained Elder in the Presbyterian Church USA. Jim is a Presidential Fellow and member of the B.T. Roberts Society at Roberts Wesleyan College where he has served on various alumni and advisory groups. Jim lived in Victor, NY for many years before moving to Sun City Hilton Head, SC in 2005.